PENGUIN BOOKS

STRIPTEASE

1853

GEORGES SIMENON

D1513345

GEORGES SIMENON

STRIPTEASE

*

TRANSLATED BY
ROBERT BRAIN

PENGUIN BOOKS

IN ASSOCIATION WITH
HAMISH HAMILTON

Penguin Books Ltd, Harmondsworth, Middlesex
AUSTRALIA: Penguin Books Pty Ltd, 762 Whitehorse Road,
Mitcham, Victoria

—

First published 1958
This translation first published by Hamish Hamilton 1959
Published in Penguin Books 1963

—

Copyright © Georges Simenon, 1958

—

Made and printed in Great Britain
by C. Nicholls & Company Ltd
Set in Monotype Garamond

PART ONE

Chapter 1

CÉLITA was the first to see the new girl.

As usual, at three o'clock in the afternoon, she had heard the alarm-clock go off on the little table between the two beds, and curling up in the sheets she had left Marie-Lou to stop the bell ringing, and next to get up and open the shutters, bring in the nylons and brassières which were drying on the window ledge, and then light the small kitchen gas-stove to make coffee.

Marie-Lou liked to sleep naked and always spent a long time wandering around the three small rooms of the flat, even when the windows were open, without dreaming of putting on any clothes. There was no sun today: the sky was overcast, the light glaucous, which meant it would rain.

'Aren't you ever going to get up?'

When, for reasons of economy, they had first decided to share the flat, they planned to take it in turns getting the breakfast, but, confronted with Célita's complete inertia, Marie-Lou had resigned herself to doing it almost every day.

In the morning her skin had an oily look, and it was perhaps because of that that she looked somehow fatter, cruder, particularly as the light exaggerated her skin's irregularities, the bluish patch under her arms where she shaved and a brown wart just below her left breast. Like many fat people, she felt no embarrassment as she traipsed from the bedroom to the dining-room and the narrow kitchen, indifferent to the fact that her heavy nakedness could be seen from the windows opposite.

That day Célita could only be bothered to have a quick shower, and with her hair tied in a pony tail she hurriedly pulled on her clothes which had been scattered on the chairs and over the floor.

'Going out?'

'I've got to sew up my red dress. Some dolt ripped it again

7

last night, trying to grab hold of me as I went past him.'

This meant that Marie-Lou would be left to do the house-work all on her own again, just as she had been left to get the breakfast. All Célita did was to fetch the milk and bread from outside the door.

The fat girl hardly ever complained, and Célita, instead of showing any gratitude, rather despised her for it; once she said to Natasha:

'She's still nothing but a chambermaid at heart!'

Marie-Lou had indeed been a housemaid for more than three years.

Célita walked briskly through the Cannes streets where people had already begun the second half of their day; she wore a thin pair of ballerina shoes, a green coat thrown across her shoulders.

She made a detour to buy a piece of red silk, and in the small triangular square in front of the church of Notre-Dame she was held up by a crowd of curious onlookers drawn up in two ranks for a wedding group to pass between. She watched with the rest, even raised herself on tiptoe to do so.

The bride was wearing a white dress with a train and a veil, and the groom, in a morning suit, held a top hat in his hand, just as in the photographs you see in magazines.

From within the half-darkness of the church the rumbling of the organ could be heard, and suddenly some girls ran forward to fling handfuls of rice at the couple who were being kept on the steps by the photographers, and all the time the women outside were dabbing at their eyes with handkerchiefs.

Did she suddenly feel outside all this, or was it only a moment of depression that affected her? Her eyelids felt hot and began to smart, and just when everything and everyone about her was becoming blurred, she recognized, in the row of faces opposite her, the man with grey hair whom she had noticed two or three times at the Monico, although he had never spoken to her. She didn't even know whether he lived in the town or if he was a tourist; all he had done was to sit on a barstool and stare at her.

Nevertheless she was certain he had just recognized her,

even with her hair untidy and no make-up on, and further-more that he had seen signs of an emotion of which she now felt ashamed.

She hated him looking at her like that, so kindly, almost pitying her, and she felt like poking her tongue out at him, then walked away from the line of people, crossly, shoving aside those next to her, so that they followed her with their eyes.

The Monico was only a couple of hundred yards away, not far from the harbour, in a narrow street crowded with cars which were parked there all day. The door was open and when Célita pulled the door curtain aside, she found the two char-women, Madame Blanc and old Madame Touzelli, sweeping up the paper streamers and little coloured balls, the atmos-phere still saturated with champagne and whisky.

Above the garnet-red benches, the window, which was always hidden in the evenings by heavy curtains, was now wide open and the cabaret stage in daylight looked as incon-gruous as Marie-Lou's nakedness when she made the coffee in their flat.

Célita had been surprised that the *patron*, Monsieur Léon, wasn't there when she came in, since most of his afternoons were spent at the Monico; when she pushed open the door leading to the cloakroom at the end of the bar, she saw the trap-door open and realized he was busy in the cellar.

She climbed the spiral staircase, which she had climbed up and down countless times in the last few months, and reached the empty, low-ceilinged room which the girls used as their dressing-room.

She rarely went there during the day and it was strange to see the yard below where a man from the brewery was stack-ing barrels. Dresses hung from a rod, in different colours and different styles; she unhooked hers, a red Spanish dancer's one, and throwing her coat off her shoulders, she sat down on a stool and started sewing.

After a while, she thought of Natasha and of the box of American face-powder a naval officer had brought her. The expensive-looking box stood on the long dressing-table where all the girls kept their personal things, and Célita opened the window, emptied her own powder-box out into the yard, then filled it to the brim with Natasha's powder.

She didn't stop to ask herself if it was unhappiness or sheer bad temper, yet her face, now that she was sewing again, was as clouded as the sky. She knew that it made her features even more pointed, her eyes more cunning, that she looked like an animal, frightened by a storm, ready to scratch. She hated sewing, just as she hated housework. In fact there were quite a number of things she hated doing! . . .

She heard a noise downstairs, and through an odd kind of fanlight which had been fitted flush with the floor she saw the *patron* and Émile in the cloakroom, climbing up from the cellar, each of them carrying bottles of whisky.

'Stack them in the cupboard. . . .' Monsieur Léon said.

He put his down on the table, pushed open the bar door, while Émile, noticing Célita looking through the pane of glass, gave a smile of happy surprise and winked at her.

Célita was aware what went on in the basement: they had both been filling empty whisky bottles with contraband whisky. It was none of her business, but she would not be very upset if the *patron* were caught, for she loathed cheats. If she cheated a bit herself, it was because she had to and she loathed herself for it.

There was no point in thinking about it. She finished her work and bit off the thread with her teeth. The skirt, which she had worn every evening for the past three years, was becoming threadbare and would not last much longer. Its red colour looked faded in the daylight. Émile was signing to her from below, but she couldn't make out what he wanted and she half-opened the door to ask him:

'What is it?'

He put his finger to his lips, beckoned her to come down quietly.

He was seventeen, but short and puny, so that he looked fifteen and everybody treated him like a little boy. It was he who helped Monsieur Léon in the afternoons, ran errands and finished up darting from car to car, slipping behind the windscreen-wipers brochures extolling the Monico's floor-show.

In the evenings, and up till four o'clock in the morning, he would wait on the pavement outside the night club, opening car doors, ushering in customers, floating in a uniform which was much too big for him.

At present he was standing in front of a small window let into the door like a peep-hole, through which one might see what was going on in the main room.

Célita had missed the beginning, but not much of it, to judge from the conversation she overheard. The two char-women were still cleaning. In the centre of the stage, bright with the daylight from outside, stood a young girl, intimi-dated, not the sort of girl one expected to find here so much as, for instance, amongst the people who had been watching the wedding a while ago.

Monsieur Léon was leaning on the bar, his jacket off and his shirt sleeves rolled up above his hairy wrists, and he was appraising the new girl with a slow, heavy look.

'Who sent you here?'

'Nobody did, sir. I just came on my own.'

Émile gave Célita a nudge with his elbow; he had moved aside to make room for her at the peep-hole and was obviously pleased to feel her so close to him.

'You come from Bergerac, you say?'

'Yes, monsieur.'

'And you heard about the Monico in Bergerac?'

'No. I haven't come straight from there.'

She wore a very simple black dress, a red hat, and she had put on a pair of white string gloves, as if she were going to Mass.

'Tell me.'

'Tell you what?'

'Where you've been before you landed up here.'

'I went to Toulouse first; there's a cabaret there called the Moulin Bleu.'

'I know the one. Did you work there?'

'No.'

11

'Why not?'

She hesitated, blushed, fiddled nervously with her black patent-leather handbag, which looked new and strangely incongruous compared to her other things.

'They didn't want me.'

'You really are nineteen?'

'I can show you my identity card.'

Her fingers fumbling through nervousness, she opened her bag as if she was not yet used to it, and held the identity card out to the *patron*, who read, half-aloud:

'Maud Leroy, born May 13th . . .'

'You see! . . .'

'I see. And after Toulouse?'

'I went to Marseilles by train and worked as a waitress in a bar for a week.'

'Which one?'

'Freddy's Bar.'

'Have you been to bed with Freddy?'

Émile gave another nudge with his elbow; Monsieur Léon seemed more than ever like an enormous cat playing with a mouse.

'Who told you that?'

'Freddy's a friend of mine. And before that?'

'What do you mean?'

'How many men had you slept with?'

She was obviously telling the truth when she answered: 'Two.'

Célita realized that her breast was crushing into Émile's shoulder, but she didn't move.

'Did Freddy tell you about me?'

'No. It was a customer. And as I left Bergerac because I wanted to become a striptease dancer . . .'

'Why?'

Disconcerted by the question, she could not think of an answer.

'Do you think it's an easy thing to do?'

'I think I could do it.'

'When did you arrive in Cannes?'

12

'I came this morning on the night train. I called here once before, at eleven, but the door was locked. I've taken a room at the Hôtel de la Poste.'

'Take your dress off.'

'Now?'

He answered with a shrug of his shoulders and the new girl looked anxiously at the two charwomen, who were apparently taking no notice of her.

'What are you waiting for?'

'Nothing . . .'

At last she made up her mind, and first put her handbag down on the table. She managed to force a smile on to her lips, and slowly, keeping her eyes glued to Monsieur Léon, she began to take off her black dress, over her head, just as she would have done in her bedroom.

'Never over your head. The other way. A woman with her arms in the air and her head inside a dress looks plain awkward.'

'I didn't know.'

'You'll learn.'

'Do I have to take my petticoat off too?'

Émile took advantage of this to press even harder against Célita, as if he wanted to see better, and she pretended not to notice.

The young girl's petticoat had fallen around her feet, and now she only wore brassière and pants; her bare skin was an almost chalky white against the night club's sombre red walls; Célita began to resent the clandestine nature of this undressing in broad daylight, with the street noises coming in through the window.

'You don't shave your armpits?'

'Do I have to?'

'Of course you have to! Let's have a look at your breasts.'

Her nipples were still smooth and bright pink. Leaning heavily on the bar, Monsieur Léon looked more like a horse-dealer than a *voyeur*, yet Célita couldn't help muttering:

'Filthy bastard!'

At the same moment she shifted a little away from Émile,

13

who, in embarrassment, stopped looking through the peep-hole with quite the same concentration.

'You can put your clothes on now.'

'Wasn't I any good?'

'I told you to put your clothes on. Have you read the notice by the door?'

As she adjusted the straps of her petticoat, she nodded her head.

'Every Friday, in addition to our usual show, we have a striptease competition for amateurs. Come along here a bit before ten o'clock, and sit down at this table . . .'

He pointed to a table at the front, near the band.

'Behave as if you were a customer and when the compère invites you, stand up as if you were hesitating. Do you get it?'

'And afterwards?'

'Don't worry about that. That's up to me. If it comes off, you're hired.'

When she had her clothes on again, she looked more than ever like any innocent young girl and it was hard to believe that she had just stripped, without a murmur.

'Thank you.'

'That's all right. Ten o'clock at the latest.'

'Yes.'

'Without fail.'

'Without fail.'

Just as she pulled the velvet curtain aside to go out, he called her back roughly:

'Have you got any money for supper?'

She turned around, blushed again.

'I don't need anything.'

'How much money have you got left?'

'Two hundred francs.'

'You'd better take this on account.'

He held out a five-hundred-franc note which she slipped into her handbag.

Émile had already moved away on tiptoe. Célita went back up the iron staircase to fetch her handbag, and when she passed through the main room, the *patron* was listening to the

14

racing results on a small wireless hidden behind the counter.

'Where have you been?'

'Upstairs. I came in to sew up my Spanish skirt.'

He studied her suspiciously; they knew each other well and he was used to her lying.

'There'll be a new girl in tonight,' he announced, as if to test her.

'So much the better: it was getting a bit dull. Dancer?'

'Striptease.'

'Has Madame Florence engaged her?'

It was a low trick, reminding him that it was his wife, whom everybody called Madame Florence, who was the real boss.

He didn't answer, but if the bar had not been between them, he might easily have slapped her. It had happened before, and yet he was incapable of doing without her. And would Célita, for her part, have been glad to do without him?

At that moment she despised and hated him, because she was scared, as she was each time a new girl appeared, as scared as Madame Florence was also.

She went out without saying good-bye and retraced her steps to the Place du Commandant-Maria, where she lived with Marie-Lou. Marie-Lou had finished tidying up the flat and was now stretched out on the sofa, filing her nails.

'There's going to be a new girl tonight.'

'Who?'

'Nobody. Just a kid who turned up here by train this morning.'

'She'll be like the rest of them.'

She wasn't the first, and no doubt she wouldn't be the last, to be tried out this way. Some of them only stayed for a single evening, and there had even been one who had panicked at the last moment before walking on to the floor, and had run and locked herself in the lavatory.

Most of them wanted to go even further than the professionals and were so clumsy and crude about it that it became obscene and made the clients feel uneasy. Two or three had kept it up for a few days. One, a little Italian girl, had got herself installed in a suite at the Carlton by the end of a week.

'Did you see her?'

'Yes.'

After a silence, during which Marie-Lou went on filing her nails, the fat girl murmured:

'Is that all?'

'What are you getting at?'

'I'm just surprised you've got nothing nasty to say about her.'

'Thanks.'

'It's a pleasure.'

These two understood each other as well.

At half past eight, wearing the dresses they always wore for dancing with clients of the club between numbers, they were mingling with the crowds in front of brightly lit shop-windows, walking precariously on their high heels. For most of the passers-by the day was over. A few couples, one or two families, were going into the cinema.

They found Natasha and Ketty already sitting down to supper at Justin's bar-restaurant in the Place du Marché; they also shared a flat, for the same reasons of economy.

'Spaghetti, Justin!' Célita called out as she walked past the zinc counter.

They ate here almost every evening and were well known to the other customers, mostly shop-keepers from the neighbourhood and, during the night, lorry-drivers, butchers, peasants who brought their vegetables to market in small trucks.

It was Marie-Lou's turn to announce the news this time:

'It seems there's a new girl.'

Oddly enough they looked at Célita, as if she would inevitably know all about it.

'What's she like?' asked Natasha.

And Célita, pursing her lips:

'Just the sort to send one of us packing. We'll soon see who.'

It was drizzling now, and as the pavement was not very wide, they walked two by two, like schoolgirls, along the wet road, their heads lowered, not talking. When they turned the street corner it was half past nine, and the Monico's sign was still not alight. Nevertheless there was a middle-aged man standing there with his face pressed up against the glass of the display box, staring at the photographs by the gleam of the street-lamp.

The four women were about thirty yards away from him when the sign and the box containing the photos were suddenly illuminated. The man, revealed by the light, jumped back, surprised, ashamed, and strode hurriedly away.

'Did you see that?' Marie-Lou inquired.

'What of it?'

'Nothing.'

Émile burst out of the door, wearing a uniform with epaulettes and braid on it, and stationed himself on the kerb. Inside, Madame Florence was already at the cash-desk, while Ludo the barman was arranging his bottles on the shelves.

'Good evening, Madame Florence.'

'Good evening.'

'Good evening, Madame Florence ...'

'Good evening ...'

They filed past her, as if past the Mother Superior at a convent, and they felt the same schoolgirl fears. The musicians were tuning their instruments.

'Marie-Lou!'

'Yes, madame.'

'Your nails? ...'

Triumphantly, Marie-Lou held out her newly manicured hands; the day before, Madame Florence had remarked on her dirty nails.

'And your hair?'

It was visibly greasy, and, on looking closer, you could see little white specks of dandruff.

'I couldn't get an appointment at the hairdresser's today. I'll go tomorrow.'

'Without fail, then.'

Natasha and Ketty were going through the cloakroom, and Célita was about to follow them when she was also called back.

'Célita!'

'Yes, Madame Florence.'

'It seems you were here this afternoon?'

Émile would never have told her; Émile worshipped Célita with a schoolboy's ardour. When he had called her down to look through the window with him that afternoon, it was more through a desire to feel her close to him than to let her share in the fun.

And considering their relationship, it would not have been in Léon's interest to say anything either.

Had Madame Florence called in at the Monico before the two cleaning-women had gone home? She often did, and somehow or other nothing escaped her.

'I forgot to take my skirt home with me yesterday. A customer grabbed hold of it and tore it. I came in to sew it up again.'

Unlike Marie-Lou, Célita did not look down at the floor, but straight at Madame Florence, with even a slightly mocking twist at the corner of her lips.

'See that it doesn't happen again.'

'Very well, Madame Florence.'

The irony was obvious. It was a kind of game they had been playing for months. But it was still difficult to pick the eventual winner. The only positive thing at present was that one of them was the *patronne*, Monsieur Léon's legal wife, and the other was not.

'Well, why are you standing there?'

'I didn't know you had finished.'

Madame Florence could not fail to know of her husband's visits to the Place du Commandant-Maria, on the afternoons when Marie-Lou was out shopping. Léon, certainly, had done the same with others, with nearly all of them, in fact, but this time it had lasted longer, it was somehow different.

He took no notice of Célita at the Monico, or if he did, it was almost always to nag her. Yet he didn't do so to put

18

Madame Florence on the wrong scent, but probably because he often found himself hating the dancer.

Outside in the street, Émile rushed forward, a red umbrella in his hand, towards a motor-car which had stopped, and he was on the point of opening the door when the driver, who was only lighting a cigarette, drove off again. Disappointed, he went back to his post by the entrance, whence he could hear the music from the band. It was rather like fishing. Some days were good, some bad. And every time a car came round the corner of the street, Émile felt the same little tug at his heart as a fisherman feels when his float sinks.

'The show will be starting right away, ladies and gentle-men. . . .'

'When does that mean?'

He never dared lie too openly. The show itself rarely started before midnight, sometimes later if there were not enough people.

Some of them pulled aside the red curtain, and when they saw the empty room, turned away, in spite of the fact that the band would strike up, as if at a signal.

'We'll come back later . . .'

'You'd better book a table . . .'

On the other hand, a miracle sometimes happened and in the space of a few minutes the place was so full that clients were jammed around the bar.

In their dressing-room upstairs the four women were putting on their make-up; Natasha, almost at once, turned to Célita and asked:

'Was it you who pinched my powder?'

Célita didn't answer. The others paid hardly any attention to them.

'If you'd only asked me I'd have given you some. But . . .'

She grabbed hold of Célita's handbag, took out her powder-case and threw the contents in the waste-paper basket, on top of a pile of soiled pieces of cotton-wool.

Her action provoked no protest from Célita, who simply gave her a hard, penetrating look as she went on brushing her hair.

Somebody was hurrying along outside, along the dark street, the rhythmic sound of her high heels disturbing the silence of the night. Émile looked at his watch, and when the woman passed him, he murmured with a touch of anxiety in his voice:

'Hurry up, Mademoiselle Francine!'

She was a pretty girl, plump and fresh, with curly hair. She went no further than the bar and was aware that everybody was staring at her: Ludo, the musicians, Jules the waiter, who was placing champagne buckets on the tables.

'I'm terribly sorry, Madame Florence. I'm a bit late ...'

'Eleven minutes.'

Without waiting, the *patronne* had taken a notebook from the drawer, with a list of names of all the employees, some of them with crosses after them.

'It's because the woman next door, the one who keeps an eye on my little boy in the evenings, hadn't come home and I couldn't leave Pierrot ...'

'I'm sorry, Francine.'

A cross was added to three others already there, each of which meant five hundred francs off Francine's wages.

'I ran as quickly as I could ...'

It was true. She was still panting.

'Go and take your coat off.'

Francine was not a singer or a dancer, performed no part in the show. She was a dance-hostess and, on top of that, was in charge of the cloakroom, hanging up customers' coats and hats in the recess.

Monsieur Léon arrived at five to ten and sat on a stool at the bar, looking around to make sure that everything was in order.

'Are the hats ready?' he asked Jules, the waiter.

Every evening they handed out party hats made of paper and cardboard, sometimes cowboy hats, sometimes sailors' berets or top-hats in all sorts of colours.

'Do you think she'll come?' his wife asked; he had told her about the new girl.

'I'm certain she will.'

Eventually Émile led in two clients, who were going to sit at the bar, when Francine rushed up to show them to a table. Once there, they were practically caught.

Almost immediately afterwards, Maud Leroy, the girl who had come that afternoon, pushed her way through the double thickness of red velvet and stood there a moment, confused, finding some difficulty recognizing the room.

Madame Florence was also a little taken aback, for the new girl was not the sort they were used to at the Monico. With a frown, she glanced at her husband out of the corner of her eye, as if she were trying to puzzle something out.

It was Ludo, the barman, who called out:

'There's a good table in the front, mademoiselle.'

Another client appeared, a regular, who sat down on the stool at the end of the bar, his back to the wall.

'A scotch, Ludo.'

'Coming up, doctor.'

He called almost all of them 'doctor', and some were flattered by it.

Madame Florence half-opened the door of the cloak-room, just next to the cash-desk, and called up the iron stair-case:

'Are you ready there?'

Instantly there was a sound of activity. Natasha and Ketty came down first. As she started down the stairs, Marie-Lou asked:

'Did you really pinch her powder?'

Célita looked at her expressionlessly, and merely shrugged her shoulders.

Downstairs the new girl was sitting bolt upright at her table, in front of a glass of yellowish liquid which had auto-matically been brought for her. Ketty, who was almost as fat as Marie-Lou, though more aggressive, more sensually coarse, walked over to the two men.

'Isn't anybody going to ask me to dance?'

Natasha, standing near the bar, waited to follow her.

21

Célita and Marie-Lou came in next, and all that now remained to be done was to 'get in tune', to create the right atmosphere.

Émile, triumphant, suddenly flung aside the curtain and let in, not one couple, but three couples at once, a party of Dutch people, terribly sunburnt in spite of the dull weather of the last few days.

Five minutes later, Gianini, the band-leader, was barking out the words of the tunes' refrains through his megaphone, and everybody was dancing on the tiny floor, colliding with each other.

At half past eleven, three-quarters of the tables were occupied, and Madame Florence called out in a low voice, giving the signal:

'Ketty! Marie-Lou!'

It was time for them to go and dress for their numbers, while downstairs the other two, plus Francine, carried on as dancing partners right up to the last moment.

Only the new girl had not danced, and none of the clients had yet dared address a word to her.

The girls had been able to examine her at their leisure as they danced or drank at the bar; so had the musicians, and Ludo, the barman, who had sent drinks across to her three times. She had drunk them mechanically, for the sake of appearances, and although she still sat as stiffly on her chair as during a sermon in church, her face was not quite so pale.

Madame Florence, without missing a thing that happened in the room, had looked across at Léon more often than usual.

She would soon be forty and the struggle was becoming too much for her.

Chapter 2

SHE was curled up in bed like a gun-dog, the sheet twisted around her body to such an extent that all that could be seen of her was a mass of tawny hair, one temple, one eye staring at the strips of light through the shutters. Occasionally her glance, turning without a sound or a move on her part, shifted to the next bed, or to the alarm-clock, although its dial faced the other way.

Célita did not know what time it was, but she was sure that the bell would soon start ringing, and when at last it did and the legs of the alarm-clock began to vibrate on the marble-topped table, she shut her eyes at once and at the same time her face assumed an exaggerated expression of innocent, yet sulky sleep, while Marie-Lou's heavy warm body slowly came to life and her arm reached out in semi-darkness.

Without looking, Célita knew her friend was sitting on the edge of her bed, her feet fumbling around on the floor for her slippers, and then, rubbing her breasts and waist, wandering out of the bedroom to the kitchen to light the gas-stove which made its usual little pop.

When Marie-Lou had opened the windows and the shutters in the dining-room, sunshine invaded the flat and the noises from the Place du Commandant-Maria became more distinct.

Between her barely parted eyelashes Célita watched the fat girl, who returned to the room after leaning out of the window, grabbed a gaudy dressing-gown which she wrapped around her before setting off again, raised her head and called out:

'Is Pierrot better?'

She was speaking to Francine, who lived in the house opposite, on the second floor; her boy had been away from school with a cold.

'What did you say?' Marie-Lou called again, after a silence; the din made by a lorry had drowned the reply.

23

Francine repeated herself, adding:

'He's at school. I was waiting for you to get up to ask you to do me a favour.'

There was a dairy at the corner and any customers there would be noticing, through the bead curtain, these two women who were just getting up at three o'clock in the afternoon.

'What kind of favour?'

'Could you look after him for me between four and six?'

Francine's five-year-old son quite often came and spent the afternoon at Marie-Lou and Célita's flat, or else one of them took him on the beach.

He was big for his age, with red cheeks and yellow hair; he would have looked pudding-faced or sleepy but for the sparkle which could be seen through the narrow slits of his eyelids.

'I'm sorry,' Marie-Lou answered. 'I can't today. I've got an appointment at the hairdresser's.'

'What about Célita?' the distant voice asked.

Through the open door between the two rooms, Marie-Lou glanced at the bed and saw the dishevelled head on the pillow. She lowered her voice and, with a gesture of her hand which must have meant something, replied:

'Better not ... You understand? ...'

Francine must indeed have understood, since she didn't press the matter.

'I've got to go inside now ... The water's boiling. ...'

Célita continued to pretend she was sleeping and soon smelt the coffee being made. She heard the door open, the crack of a thin length of bread being broken, a cup clink against a saucer.

Marie-Lou was taking care not to wake her, and Célita, for her part, was not going to make the first move; so she remained in bed, quite still.

She had a guilty conscience, but, instead of owning up, she was feeling bitter towards her friend for what she considered to have been a betrayal. The night before, or rather that morning, as they came home from the Monico together, Marie-Lou hadn't once opened her mouth, and she had un-

24

dressed straight away and gone to bed without saying good night.

It was going to be worse with the others, Célita was expecting it. Anyway, they hated her already. A little more or less, what did it matter? . . .

And was the celebrated Maud, the new girl, also waking up at this moment in her bedroom at the Hôtel de la Poste? Had Monsieur Léon already been to knock at her door?

Madame Florence was the only one who had not reacted like the rest, and for a brief moment, as Célita's eyes chanced to meet hers, a look of understanding, tinged with complicity, had passed between them.

Although their positions were dissimilar, they would both defend themselves, and in either case it was over the same man.

Nothing had been premeditated. Célita had only done it on the spur of the moment, although she was admittedly aware that she was playing a dirty trick. She was not drunk. She had had three or four glasses of whisky at the most, and, God knows, the ones Ludo poured were short measure, particularly when he served the hostesses.

A few minutes before midnight, having peered through the peep-hole to make sure Ketty was ready in the cloakroom, Madame Florence had given Gianini the signal. When the dance ended, there was a drum-roll followed by a crash on the cymbals and then he made his usual speech:

'Ladies and gentlemen, the management of the Monico has the greatest pleasure in presenting to you their striptease review, the most daring, the most artistic show in all the Riviera. To begin with, here is Mademoiselle Ketty, the incomparable cover-girl, in her original number . . .'

At that moment Célita was sitting at the bar with a young Englishman who had bought her a drink, but would not dance.

As usual, the place had been plunged into absolute darkness for Ketty's number. The first flash of the photographer's flare revealed her swathed in black silk, like a girl posing for a magazine cover, a long cigarette-holder in her hand.

Darkness. Flash. Darkness... Each time, Ketty was sitting in the same place, slightly more undressed, until she finally appeared completely naked except for the regulation g-string.

The Englishman only bothered to give her a quick look and went on talking in laboured French about night clubs in London where you couldn't buy a drink after eleven o'clock in the evening.

'And now, ladies and gentlemen ...'

Marie-Lou's turn: her number was cruder and more ordinary. She was also dressed in black. Her dress, her corset, her underclothes were all fastened by zips, which she invited the customers to undo.

'You're next, Célita. ...'

She excused herself to the Englishman, walked through the small cloakroom, climbed the iron staircase. Natasha was already busily completing the last stages of a flashy get-up, in the style of the early 1900s, topped by a hat trimmed with ostrich feathers.

They could hear snatches of the music and the applause.

Célita went down first in her Spanish costume and, as they each did in turn, watched the end of the previous act through the peep-hole; Marie-Lou was also now naked, wearing only a g-string like Ketty, except that hers was covered with spangles, and she was walking across the floor for the last time before taking her leave and collecting her clothes.

When she pushed open the door, breathless, her body was hot, shining with sweat.

'Your go ...'

'And now, ladies and gentlemen, I have the pleasure ...'

She had heard those phrases so many times before that she now failed to distinguish the individual words, and like the horses at the circus, she waited for the first bars of music before going on to the floor.

As she danced a flamenco, at the end of which she would lose her bodice and red skirt, Célita noticed that the Englishman had disappeared, then, a little later, that the new girl, in her corner, was staring fixedly into space.

Célita was the only trained dancer; her mother had enrolled

her at a dancing school in Paris when she was eight, and she had been a member of several corps de ballet. She was also the only one not to expose her breasts, even though hers were firmer and higher than Marie-Lou's, for example. Nor did she have the g-string clinging to the skin of her abdomen, but, both for the Spanish dances and for the can-can, she wore linen pants with flounces.

The club was full for a Friday and already there was a blanket of smoke hovering overhead, and the comic hats had been distributed. During the show Monsieur Léon was in his usual position near the door, where he encouraged the applause.

Had Célita won her struggle with him? He was beginning to think so; she fervently hoped so.

Their eyes met for an instant, but she couldn't read anything in his look, apart from a certain impatience, and she was convinced it was on account of Maud.

Like Marie-Lou a little earlier, she hurried off towards the cloakroom, brushing past Natasha, who was waiting for her cue, holding a very long-handled mauve parasol.

Marie-Lou was already downstairs, sitting at the table with the two men who had arrived first; they had offered her a drink at last. In the dressing-room, Ketty was also getting ready to go down and she merely said:

'Quite a crowd!'

If there were enough people left at two o'clock, they would have to put on a second show and the whole thing would start again, with Gianini making the same announcements, the girls going up and down the same iron staircase, getting dressed and undressed all over again, excuses to be made as they parted from clients who might or might not be there on their return.

She put on her hostess's dress, which was getting worn too, went down, watched, from the cloakroom, the end of Natasha's number, the most intricate and sophisticated of them all. Natasha had a beautiful body, but she was so tall that she looked more like a statue in a square than a woman you would take to bed. Célita hadn't thought that one up. It was a remark made by an Italian client who came to Cannes once a month to gamble at the Casino and only appeared in the Monico when he had lost money up to a self-imposed limit earlier in the evening.

Another drum-roll, a crash on the cymbals, followed by an almost solemn silence, during which Célita slipped into the room and remained standing near the door.

'This is Friday night, ladies and gentlemen, and every Friday we have our amateur striptease competition ... The management of the Monico is convinced that among our charming spectators there are hidden talents, women and young girls who are burning with the desire to start a career of ...'

Each week the same old words, the same winks, the same pauses which Gianini had perfected once and for all. The lights were put out and replaced by a spotlight which searched the room while the compère poured out his patter; it stopped from time to time at certain tables, emphatically or merely glancingly, revealing now a face, now a bosom, sometimes legs interlinked.

'Let's see which girl or young lady is going to win the bottle of champagne the management has kindly presented ... You, madame?'

He knew he would get a good laugh if he chose one of the lobster-faced Dutch women, who giggled like a child, while her husband teased her, pretending to push her forward.

Célita didn't take her eyes off Maud during all this. Maud who sat completely still, her lips drained of all colour, her nostrils pinched, seeming to have stopped breathing.

Célita was aware that she wasn't the only one watching her in this way; Madame Florence at the cash-desk, and the *patron* at the door, were no less attentive, although for different reasons.

At one moment the young girl put her hand out to her bag, as if she were going to seize it and rush into the street. Jules, working the spotlight, must have noticed this movement and suspected the danger, because the light was suddenly swung on to her.

28

Gianini saw that the time had come.

'You, mademoiselle? . . .'

Like a hunted animal, she remained perfectly still.

'Will you tell me your christian name?'

Her lips moved, but there was not the slightest sound.

'What did you say? . . . Hortense? . . . Ursule? . . . Pélagie? . . .'

This time the people at the next table heard her murmur something and one of them repeated in a loud voice:

'Maud.'

'What a pretty name, Maud! . . . Well now, Mademoiselle Maud . . . You aren't married, I suppose? . . .'

Did she know what was happening to her? She shook her head, mechanically.

'Will you oblige the ladies and gentlemen by standing up? Then we can all see just how nice you are.'

She got to her feet, with an abrupt jerk.

'That's fine! Perfect! You see, you're getting used to it already. Don't be scared. The rest will come quite naturally. How old are you, Maud?'

'Nineteen.'

'Nineteen! How marvellous! I want all the other nineteen-year-olds in the audience to raise their little fingers! . . . Nobody? . . . What, sir? . . . Ninety? . . . That's not quite the same you know . . . You see, Maud, you're already in a class of your own . . . Are you engaged?'

'No.'

'Louder.'

'No!'

'Unfortunate for him, but fortunate for the rest of us, eh? Come closer, Maud . . . Don't be nervous . . . You've just been admiring our pretty girls doing their acts, and now you're going to show us that you needn't have done it for years to be good at it . . .'

In spite of his glibness and his teasing, he was following all the girl's reactions carefully and he sensed in time her mounting panic. He made a sign to the band and they understood. After a crash from the bass drum, heavy, rhythmic music accompanied him as he went on talking, insistently, like a hypnotist:

'Come just another two steps closer, Maud . . . Two steps . . . I said two steps . . . Of course you can! . . . You see? . . . Very good . . . Ladies and gentlemen, Mademoiselle Maud is now going to perform for you her first striptease act . . .'

He conducted the band with both hands now, and they played with a strong beat, haunting chords, while the spotlight, turning red, enveloped Maud in a suggestive glow.

The first time, the newcomer, with her eyes glued to Gianini, lifted her hands to her shoulders to slip off her dress, but her arms fell down again, weakly, standing out white beside her body.

He smiled at her, urging her on, still beating time with his hands as if he were carving strange shapes in the air.

Suddenly she glanced fearfully across at the door where, through a fog of smoke, she saw the *patron*'s gaze fixed on her.

The whole thing was becoming painful and somebody at a table opened his mouth to call out:

'That's enough! . . .'

At that moment Célita was feeling as embarrassed as the rest, waiting for something that just wasn't happening. Weren't they all conscious of taking part in some cruel game?

Her hands were rising again, pink and pale, her fingers stretched the straps of her black dress so that they parted to reveal, first, the polished nakedness of her round shoulders, then the hollows of her armpits, her still thin arms.

Her body remained motionless, stiff, while the dress slowly slipped down till, having passed her hips, it fell suddenly around her feet.

One person alone started applauding from a corner. Another hissed: 'Ssssh! . . .'

Perhaps the music, like a sort of voodoo incantation, was having a soothing effect on the audience's taut nerves, for no one spoke or touched his glass; everybody's eyes, without an exception, converged on that still unmoving silhouette in the purple spotlight.

Slowly the girl bent down and extricated her legs and then,

probably unconsciously, she did something which was almost inspired. Her hands gradually moved back up her body, caressing lovingly the silk of her stockings; then, as she took off her petticoat, she revealed her body little by little, a body which somehow looked more intimate than that of any of the other girls who had just preceded her.

Even Gianini was holding his breath now, careful not to break the spell she was casting, trying to match the girl's gestures with his music, encouraging, even provoking them.

Célita hurt herself as her pointed teeth bit into her lips. Twice, three times, she thought, she hoped, that Maud would panic at the last minute, that she would suddenly break off, see the faces watching her, and run away.

Nothing like that happened. Ignoring Monsieur Léon's instructions, the girl took off her petticoat over her head; it was like a sudden deliverance: the feeling of her near-nakedness was like a slap in her face; you could see the blood rush to her cheeks, as she now took her eyes off the band-leader and dared, at last, to search the darkened room.

There were sighs of relief, particularly when she allowed a smile to flit across her face, a smile which was directed only at herself, at her own secret thoughts.

Gianini grasped the situation and accelerated the beat until the music throbbed savagely like a jungle tom-tom.

Then she began to dance. Not a trained dance. It was hardly a dance at all, strictly speaking, but the movements, still hesitant, of a being who was slowly coming to life.

Throughout, everybody could feel that the whole thing was suspended on a thread, that the slightest thing, a cough, a laugh, a jolt, would be enough to break the spell.

The hardest part still remained to be done: Célita knew that better than anybody, she who had never consented to reveal her breasts in public.

A deep, long breath. A frightened, anxious look into the dark space around her, and Maud slipped one hand behind her back to unfasten her brassière.

At that instant Célita bit her lip so hard that she felt a drop of blood; she realized the new girl had just won a victory, that neither she nor any of the other girls had ever been able to hold an audience in such breathless suspense.

After another crash on the cymbals, Gianini, with beads of sweat on his forehead, abruptly changed the beat again; the instruments made the music seem to pant, hesitatingly at first, plaintively, then bit by bit almost triumphantly.

Was this what the girl from Bergerac had imagined when she left home determined to become a striptease artist? Were those looks, caressing her body, sending her into a kind of trance?

Unlike Marie-Lou, she did not merely mime the stages of love-making. She was living them, defying the people who were watching her. They could see the tremors run across her skin, and both men and women alike forgot her breasts, her stomach, her buttocks, to stare into the wild light in her eyes.

When she fell to her knees, everybody stood up, a few applauding; they were quickly silenced, for, with her eyelids half-closed, her body was sustaining a mysterious struggle until, at last, she fell down backwards, drained of all strength.

Célita had been as fascinated as the rest of them, but it only made her doubly furious, particularly when the oppressive silence was followed by an ovation which made the glasses jump on the tables; they clapped hands, stamped their feet, called out, stood on tiptoe to peer over other people's shoulders at the girl's body, now so still, as if it had been emptied of all substance.

'Ladies and gentlemen . . .'

Gianini's voice was lost in the din. Anxiously, Monsieur Léon was pushing his way through the crowd, no longer able to see anything from the door.

'Well done, my dear!'

He was so overcome that Célita and Madame Florence glanced at each other.

The *patron* was holding out his hand to Maud, helping her to get up, picked up her clothes and led her away to the door with the peep-hole.

They were still applauding and Gianini struck up a samba

which attracted some couples on to the floor where the lights had been turned on again.

Florence had left the till. She must have gone to join her husband and the girl in the passage. Natasha muttered, as she walked past:

'So you were right after all, darling. . . .'

Célita remembered that she had told them at Justin's a while ago that the new girl might take the place of one of them. She had said it to tease them, not really believing it.

Maud Leroy threatened to take not merely the place of one of them, but Célita's own particular place. Madame Florence had realized this too. It was all very well to hate each other, to fight over the same man, but none the less, in a case like this, they might join forces.

After the first show there was always a certain upheaval. Clients would ask for the bill and Jules wouldn't know which way to turn, while Francine hurried to and fro, laden with overcoats and furs.

Nobody was paying any attention to a black patent-leather handbag which was lying beside an empty glass, on the table where Maud had sat. This bag, which was so new, fascinated Célita, and she had already noticed that afternoon how it contrasted with the tired-looking clothes the girl wore.

But it was not an intuition: simply curiosity. Nothing prevented her from going and sitting at the next table; it was unoccupied and it was a place where one or other of the girls often sat. Marie-Lou was busy with her two clients. Natasha was standing at the bar trying to persuade an American to buy her a drink; he had just come in and must at first have thought everything was over.

'Bring me a scotch, Jules.'

'In a minute, Mademoiselle Célita. When I've given them their change.'

She put the bag on her lap, as if it were her own, and began searching around inside, found an enamelled-copper powder-case, a handkerchief, two letters, a tube of aspirins, some cotton-wool, and an almost empty packet of cigarettes.

What made her take one of the three cigarettes left and

light it? Sheer defiance? To pay back the new girl for the wrong she was unwittingly doing her?

She slid her fingers down the small pockets sewn into the sides of the bag and drew out a small rectangular card. Printed on it were the words: *Galeries Nouvelles*. And below, stamped in violet ink, the sum: *4450 francs*.

When Jules returned, the bag was back in its right place on the table and Célita was no longer there. She was slipping towards the exit. Émile, who was much occupied with departing clients, noticed her, but had no time to say anything.

A narrow street, too narrow for motor-cars, old houses, without a single light still shining, on either side, ran off to the right towards the Place du Marché.

A few lorries had already arrived and were beginning to be unloaded. Two men in overalls and leather caps were eating sandwiches and drinking coffee at Justin's bar.

She asked him for a *jeton* for the telephone.

He noticed she looked drawn, that her eyes were feverish, but he thought nothing of it as he watched her walk to the box.

'Hello! ... Is that the police? ... A handbag priced at four thousand, four hundred and fifty francs was stolen from the Galeries Nouvelles in the rue Foch this morning ... The thief is now at the Monico where she's just done a strip-tease act ... Her name is Maud Leroy ...'

'Who is that speaking?' a voice answered, unimpressed.

She hung up, left the box, forgetting to shut the door.

'I'll pay you later, Justin. ....'

'Have you got a crowd there?'

When she returned to the Monico, things had calmed down again and Émile, back on sentry duty, opened his mouth to ask her a question. But she slipped between the velvet curtains before he had time to speak.

Florence, at the cash-desk, frowned. The grey-haired man, whom she had noticed that afternoon watching the wedding procession, was sitting at the bar, and she went straight to work:

'Will you buy me a drink?'

'If you want me to.'

She jerked herself up on to the stool next to his.

'Thanks. A scotch, Ludo.'

'Cigarette?' her companion offered.

She took one and lit it.

'Been out for some fresh air?'

For a moment she wondered whether he was making fun of her, he was smiling at her so oddly. She had already noticed that smile of his the two or three times he had been there before; it was only a sketch of a smile and it had been enough to stop her talking to him. He was too pleased with himself; he studied people with a curiosity that seemed too compassionate.

She remembered saying to Marie-Lou:

'That one thinks he's God the Father!'

Marie-Lou had added, bantering:

'God the Father watching the girls strip!'

He was soberly dressed, in a tweed suit, and suggested a doctor or a lawyer, perhaps a professor?

Neither Monsieur Léon nor the new girl was in the room. A little later they both appeared together, and the *patron* led the girl to her table, where she found her bag; then he left her on her own and went to have a word, first with his wife, then with Gianini, who listened to him, going on quietly playing his accordion.

The amateur's trick could not be repeated at the second show because too many of the clients had stayed on who had seen it earlier.

Since Maud had not left, but had been given something to drink, it meant that she would appear with the others, although she would presumably be announced as the sensational newcomer.

Provided that ...

Célita turned and looked towards the door, wondering whether the police had taken her telephone call seriously and if they would send a detective around.

'Had a bad day?' her companion with the grey hair asked her, in a light tone.

'Why do you think that?'

'You were a bundle of nerves this afternoon. You don't much like watching others getting married, is that it?'

She went on drinking, not answering him. At the same moment Émile came in, tried to attract the *patron*'s attention, but succeeded only when it was too late and Detective-Inspector Moselli, who occasionally called to keep an eye on the Monico, was walking up to the cash-desk.

'Nothing!' Célita spat at him. 'Nothing's the matter with me, do you hear! Just what are you trying to insinuate? ...'

She realized too late that she had behaved unwisely. Everything was happening very rapidly now. At the end of the counter the inspector was speaking to Madame Florence in a low voice, and her husband had joined them. The policeman had not entered unnoticed, and people were looking in his direction, Marie-Lou, Natasha, and Francine, sitting alone at a table.

After a moment Monsieur Léon went over to Maud, who mechanically picked up her bag from the table and followed the *patron* into the small cloakroom; the inspector went in after them.

Célita expected the glance, or rather series of glances, that Madame Florence duly gave her; the first furtive, hesitant, as if the *patronne* were not yet sure what was going on. The second revealed a certain surprise as if she were thinking:

'Well, my girl, I never thought you'd be capable of going as far as that!'

An admiring glance? A little, perhaps. Are there not times when we admire, despite ourselves, people who have the courage to do harm?

She probably had an inkling that Célita was actually working for both of them. Yet Célita realized, from the resigned look on the *patronne*'s face, that her attempt would hang fire.

Natasha, always more curious than the others, was making her way to the cloakroom, pretending to be going to the lavatory.

'What's making you so scared?'

She was beginning to hate this insidious voice, the way the

36

man in the tweed suit looked at her, sarcastically and yet indulgently.

'Not you, at all events!' she answered dryly.

And she got down from her stool to go and sit with Francine.

'Did you see that?' the latter asked.

'See what?'

'The detective. He's come for the new one. I wonder what they're up to at the back.'

They were all to find out a little later. The policeman in due course came back into the room together with the *patron* and they both had a drink at the bar. Not until the inspector had gone did Maud come and sit down at her former table, holding her bag in her hand, her eyes moist and her cheeks flushed.

Natasha moved eagerly from one to another of the girls, whispering in their ears and indicating Célita with her glance.

Monsieur Léon must have handed over the money for the handbag, thus making sure they would hear no more of the matter. Had the shop even noticed the theft? It was unlikely. The strangest thing of all was that Célita, even at the moment of discovering the price-ticket, had realized the girl was not wholly guilty. She probably only had an old bag of her own, hardly presentable enough for the day she was going to take such an important step ... She only had two hundred francs left ... It was double or quits ...

For the rest of the evening, Monsieur Léon just looked right through Célita. When she went upstairs to change for the second show, Natasha ignored her, and later, outside in the street, Marie-Lou was to be equally disdainful and silent.

She knew what it meant; she was being put in quarantine, just as she had been at school.

Now Marie-Lou had finished her bath; she came into the bedroom, her body dripping, and without bothering to find out if Célita were awake or not, gathered up her underwear and clothes.

Célita preferred to keep still, her eyes shut, hoping only that her friend would not notice the two tears which were squeezing between her eyelids.

37

She wasn't even to be allowed to mind Pierrot!

She would be by herself until the evening, because Marie-Lou had put on the blue frock which she wore to go to the Monico and was obviously planning not to come home first.

The door had opened and shut, the footsteps faded away along the pavement. Célita had jumped out of bed, tempted to run and call her friend back.

She had never felt quite so lonely in the three-roomed flat, where flies were now buzzing in the sunshine and all the noises from outside seemed hostile.

She almost felt she had been caught in a trap.

She lifted the telephone receiver, dialled a number, heard it ringing at the other end of the line, then finally a hesitant voice, the voice of somebody who wasn't used to speaking on the telephone.

'Yes ...'

'Is that the Monico?'

'This is the Monico, yes ...'

She thought she recognized Madame Touzelli's mumbling voice.

'Has Monsieur Léon arrived?'

'No, madame.'

'Madame Florence is not there either?'

'There's nobody here.'

Angrily she hung up, poured herself a cup of cold coffee, had nothing to eat and ran herself a bath; she must get some clothes on as quickly as possible and go out somewhere, along the rue d'Antibes or on the Croisette, anywhere, so long as she could escape from this loneliness in the flat.

Chapter 3

SHE had hesitated a moment between her tight trousers, toreador-style, which she wore with a blouse when she went on the beach, and a dress with red spots which she had bought a week ago, at the Galeries Nouvelles, the same shop where Maud had stolen the patent-leather handbag. She had finally chosen the dress. She had made herself look pretty and smart, done her hair nicely, and set off to window-shop in the rue d'Antibes.

Cannes had been nothing but an ordinary, small provincial town during the past days, when the sky had been overcast and it had been cold. No sooner had the sun begun to shine again than it was impossible not to feel that you were on the Riviera; the tourists were invading the streets, speaking every possible language, men in shorts, like scoutmasters, revealing hairy calves, and women dressed that way as well, some of them enormously fat, others who even wandered about the pavements and into the shops in bathing-costumes, smelling of sun-tan lotion, which was almost becoming the town's distinctive smell.

Once, when Célita and Marie-Lou were out for a walk, more respectably dressed than most of the other women in the streets, two housewives had none the less turned round to look at them, guessing what sort of women they were and passing uncomplimentary remarks in voices loud enough for them to hear. It had spoiled Célita's afternoon, but Marie-Lou had only murmured, philosophically:

'Don't take any notice, darling! I don't know why we bother how we dress, they always know what we do to earn our living.'

It was true. The very day before, when the married couple were coming out of church, the other people had realized that she belonged to a different kind of world, though the only one to recognize her as the dancer from the Monico had been the man with grey hair.

She turned down a side street to go to the Croisette, perhaps because somebody was eyeing her too inquisitively. From a distance she recognized Francine, in her blue costume, on the other side of the street, walking along with a middle-aged man.

Célita knew beforehand that they would go into a boarding-house, half-way along the street, where you could hire rooms by the night, or even by the hour. Francine went in first, then the man, with his head slightly bowed; when she passed the house she looked inside, saw the gloomy corridor, the door with its frosted glass, with all of which she was too familiar.

She didn't go there very often, almost always towards the end of the month, when she hadn't enough money to pay the rent, or as last week, when she wanted a new dress.

She had never asked Léon for a thing, and he would probably never have given her anything. Yet he knew very well how she set about procuring the necessary cash, since he was more often than not the middleman when the customers wanted to proposition any of the hostesses.

Could he ever become jealous? He hadn't been so with Florence, in the days when they had both been living at Pigalle, he as a barman in a low sort of club, while she, much younger then, had unashamedly been on the game and continued doing so during his eighteen months in prison.

Nobody here really knew the story behind his conviction. It was mentioned as seldom as possible at the Monico, and then only in whispers. One of the musicians maintained that two rival gangs had had a brawl in the bar where Léon was working, with one man killed and another left seriously injured in the street, and that Léon had copped it with the rest of them. Ludo didn't hold with this story; he knew a lot about those Corsican and Marseilles gangs. Ludo claimed that the present owner of the Monico had always operated on his own, a lone wolf, whom both the gangs suspected of being in league with the police.

Whichever it was, Léon had married Florence when he came out of prison, and afterwards they had set up in business together, with both the Monico and their flat in the Boulevard

Carnot in his wife's name, as nearly always happened in such cases.

It was now some years since Madame Florence had been on the job. She was thirty-nine, almost forty. She had become middle-class and respectable, and for some time she had been looking unhealthily fat.

Célita, at thirty-two, felt she herself was already old.

Until yesterday the struggle had been between these two women, and Célita had been confident of victory. She remembered that day, during her first week at the Monico, when the *patron* had called to see her in her hotel bedroom, at the Hôtel de la Poste, as he had done with Maud. To begin with, he had seemed to think he was only getting his due, as if it were just a matter of routine.

'I suppose I have to put up with it?' she had said to him calmly, as he took off his coat and tie.

'Does it surprise you?'

He had been intrigued and taken aback by her tone of voice.

'I'm not surprised at anything any more.'

'What did you expect then?'

'Nothing.'

She had drawn the curtains and climbed into bed. The whole time she had stared at the ceiling, her body inert, her face indifferent.

'Are you doing this on purpose?'

'Perhaps.'

'Are you always so mild?'

She realized that he was put out, not so pleased with himself.

'What else would you like?'

Later as he got dressed, he had mumbled:

'You think you've been real smart, I bet.'

She had had to hide her little smile of satisfaction, because she knew now that she had chosen the right line, that he was intrigued, humiliated, and that he would come again, determined to bring her to heel.

That evening, all the others, except Natasha, who had

not yet arrived in Cannes, heard about the visit she had been paid.

'Well, did he get what he wanted?'

Marie-Lou, like a good friend, had warned her.

'Whatever happens, don't get ideas and imagine that this is it! It's just a craze of his. He's got to feel himself the boss, show he's a real man, you see? He'll probably go and see you a couple of times, just casually, but it's such a trifling affair his wife's not even jealous ...'

It was true. To judge by her attitude, Madame Florence practically went out of her way to show Célita, who was the new girl then, that she knew all about it and took no offence.

'We'll see!' Célita had replied to Marie-Lou, out of sheer bravado.

'See what?'

'Nothing.'

Had she thought up her plan even then? She couldn't say herself. More likely it had just come to her bit by bit. At first, it had been a kind of game. For her he wasn't Monsieur Léon, or even plain Léon. He was the man. And, beside him, there was Madame Florence, the woman to be ousted.

Célita had not been deaf to the mutterings that went on behind her back, and Marie-Lou, ever incapable of holding her tongue, had been less able to conceal from her that she was thinking just the same.

'You're envious, Célita. If something nice happens to other people it makes you mad, and you'd do almost anything to stop them being happy.'

This was not quite true. Once, soon after Natasha's arrival, when they were both still friends, they had had a long talk on the subject. Natasha was more intelligent than Marie-Lou or Ketty, or the other girls who had passed some time at the Monico. She used to read a lot and was the only one never to go to bed with any clients. Nobody was quite sure if she'd even let the *patron* have her.

She was married to a commercial traveller and had a child, a little girl of three. She had left her husband, and the divorce she had asked for was now being heard. She claimed custody of her daughter and any day now she expected the court's decision.

'They say I'm envious because I'm different from them.'

'Other people hate one to be different from them.'

'It's not envy with me, it's just that I loathe injustice ...'

Natasha had seemed to be sympathetic at that time, and they had nearly shared a flat together in the rue Pasteur.

'Some people get all the luck, and they're always the ones who deserve it least. Look at Marie-Lou for example; she's as stupid as the backside of a cow and everyone's nice to her. ....'

Why had Natasha tired of her? A few days later she had turned cold and deliberately avoided Célita, who had asked her openly:

'Have I done anything wrong?'

'What do you mean wrong?'

'I don't know. I just wondered why you've changed towards me.'

'You tire me.'

After a silence, she added, searching for the right words:

'You're too complicated. You try to dramatize yourself the whole time ...'

Was it her fault if drama seemed to cling to her? Hadn't she always tried to do her best, intensely, passionately?

Natasha should have understood, she knew the story of her past.

'When I was four I had to sleep with the woman next door – just like Pierrot – in the rue Caulaincourt, while my mother was dancing in night clubs, and when I was eight she sent me to a ballet school where I suffered absolute hell, dancing on my toes and dislocating every part of my body. And all that time I had a brother and sister in Hollywood, being spoiled by their wealthy parents. Do you know who my father is?'

She had told her: José Delgado, the famous singer and film star, whose photo was often in the papers.

'I was born too soon, when he was a nobody, sharing a room in Montmartre with my mother. He never married her, and left for the United States when I was two. Over there he got married three times, had other children; they say he's getting divorced again, and there'll be yet another wedding...'

'What difference does it make to you?' Natasha had retorted.

She didn't understand, and yet she could not have led a very happy life herself, having left her husband and her daughter. As for Marie-Lou, provided she no longer had to work as a maid-of-all-work and get up at six o'clock in the morning, all her problems were solved. Now and again she fell in love, which might last for three weeks or a month. The latest was a croupier from the casino who looked like an undertaker's mute.

At the age of sixteen Célita had been in the chorus of various operettas touring smaller towns and second-rate casinos, having her meals more often in trains and station snack-bars than in proper restaurants.

Nevertheless she had once had her own man, when she was twenty-two, a man with whom she lived, admittedly in a hotel room, in the Boulevard Saint-Martin, making plans for their future together. When she found out she was pregnant, she had imagined he would have shared her joy. In her third month, she was still dancing at the Châtelet.

Her friend worked in a shipping firm and she was happy to think she would soon be able to escape from the theatre. They would have a little house in the suburbs, more children, a car later on.

Everything seemed settled when a woman, a sly-looking, small brunette, who wasn't even pretty, took him from her.

'They're married now, Natasha. They're happy. They've got three children going to school ...'

'And yours?'

'Mine died. It was a little girl. Since her father had left me she was all I had.'

She paused, wanting some sympathy, at least some sign of approbation.

'Can you imagine what it was like?'

'What happened?'

'I didn't want to board her in the country. I needed to have her near me. In the evenings, like Francine, I let a woman

44

on the same floor look after her for me. Nothing's happened to Francine's little boy. Nothing will happen to him. Nothing awful ever happens to other people. When my baby was thirteen months old she was suffocated by the woman who was looking after her; she had taken her into her own bed because she was crying. She was drunk that evening, I know, because she stank of alcohol the next morning, and she hadn't noticed anything.'

'You haven't had much luck, you poor thing.'

And Célita flung back:

'It's not a matter of luck, it's a matter of justice!'

She had decided to fend for herself, to fight, if need be. Operettas were almost a thing of the past. The theatres were turning dancers away, or they wanted them young.

'I'm thirty-two. It'll soon be too late . . .'

She didn't like talking about her experiences of the last ten years.

'Before long they won't even take me as a shop-assistant at Prisunic!'

Did Marie-Lou ever worry about the future? Or Ketty? Or Natasha? Were they still hoping to find a husband, at the Monico or elsewhere?

'Nobody's ever bothered their head over me. I'm damned if I'm going to bother about other people!'

Poor Madame Florence, if Célita should succeed!

It was a three-sided struggle, because the first one to deal with was Léon himself. He wanted people to think of him as a real man, and he believed he had had a lot of experience. As far as he was concerned, the girls who came and went at the Monico were worth a visit, sometimes two, after which he couldn't care less. He did it rather as if he were a stockman branding his herd.

But, after six months, he had still not been able to leave off Célita, and he could not have explained how she managed it. She was sometimes convinced that he had guessed where her ambitions lay.

'You know, sweetheart,' he had told her the second week, 'it's no use your getting any big ideas. There's nothing doing.

45

Maybe we do go to bed together now and then, but it ends there. There are plenty of others, smarter girls than you at that, who've tried to get their clutches on me. Just ask my wife . . .'

A month later, staring into her eyes, he was questioning her, furious:

'What have you been planning inside your little head?'

She forced a laugh.

'You're the nastiest, most vicious bitch I've ever come across.'

He hated not to understand something and felt humiliated when somebody stood up to him.

'Can you ever have actually been in love with anyone?'

'It would be funny if I was just beginning to learn now . . .'

Between Madame Florence and Célita, the war was at once pettier and more cruel, made up of slight annoyances and smiling treacheries. Some months Célita had collected so many five-hundred-franc fines that at the end she got nothing, and, even in front of the clients, the *patronne* never hesitated to insult her.

Yet Célita remained and it was Florence who was frightened; only two days ago Léon had spent a couple of hours at the Place du Commandant-Maria, and for the first time he had said afterwards, just as he was going:

'It would be more convenient if you got rid of Marie-Lou and had the place to yourself . . .'

Was she imagining things or was he beginning to need her?

But now there was Maud . . .

And Maud was there, on the beach, lying in the sun near a blue parasol. Célita was making her way along the Croisette, which, almost overnight, had assumed its summer look. Here, everybody was on holiday, climbing out of motor-cars, walking about taking photos, or relaxing on the sandy beach, stretched out in their bathing-costumes.

Did these holiday-makers in their brightly coloured clothes, their bodies sunburnt to a greater or less degree, also have their worries?

At any rate there was one consolation: Maud was not with Léon in her hotel bedroom, as Célita had feared.

One of them had gone to fetch her, Ketty or Natasha. They had enrolled her in their little group straight away, and she was lying, near the parasol, in the spot usually reserved for Célita.

While his mother was at the boarding-house, Pierrot, his hair gleaming in the sun, was playing under the watchful eyes of the three young women in bikinis, as they chatted among themselves.

Ketty saw Célita first, glancing up, and pointed her out to the others. They must have been talking about her because Ketty said:

'Careful! There she is . . .'

They didn't wave to her, pretended not to have noticed her. Like them, Célita was wearing dark glasses, which made her features look hard; she walked more slowly, seemed to hesitate whether to go down on the sand, then casually sat in one of the deck-chairs near the railing, just opposite them.

Pierrot had seen her and rushed up to tell Natasha:

'Do you know Célita's up there?'

Natasha must have replied:

'Leave her alone! Don't look her way! We've got nothing to do with her.'

'Why not?'

'It doesn't matter. Don't worry your head over it.'

'Has she been naughty?'

Maud's skin was whiter than the others', and instead of a bikini she was wearing a respectable lastex bathing-costume. Pierrot was obviously not satisfied with the replies he had been given, and after staring at Célita for quite a while, screwing up his eyes because of the sun, he turned away regretfully and went to paddle in the water.

The three women, knowing they were being watched, played a little game of pretending to whisper secrets to each other with great glee.

Célita had not spent much time at school, but the same sort of thing went on at kindergarten and, later on, before and after dancing-lessons, except that the mothers also joined in then, even nastier than their daughters.

A young married couple were holding hands on a bench close by, watching the sea; perhaps they were seeing it for the first time. Meanwhile, a little further along, an old man could not take his eyes off a plump woman lying face down on the sand, who had unfastened the top part of her bikini.

The second show, the night before, had been less of a triumph for Maud than the first. She had made practically the same gestures, in the same order, but it seemed, this time, as if she didn't have her heart in it, as if she was repeating a lesson she had learnt, and just as she was about to uncover her breasts, she had stood there for a moment, lost, as if she had forgotten what was to come next, or as if she had suddenly become aware of the incongruousness of her behaviour.

Yet they had applauded her. She had not waited for the *patron* to come to her, but picked up her clothes and hurried through the door with the peep-hole. A little later Monsieur Léon had gone up to her in the dressing-room, probably to tell her not to lose heart.

He would go and see her, as he had gone to see the rest. It would be interesting to know if she could keep him returning for more than a week.

Léon must be very angry with Célita for having called the police. He had steered clear of her all evening and not said good night to her. Perhaps she had been wrong to leave the flat, where he might have gone to see her this afternoon, to reproach her for it?

The other three were keeping up their play-acting, though with less enthusiasm. Natasha called to Pierrot and gave him a bun which she had just bought from a beach vendor.

'Hello, Mademoiselle Célita.'

She jumped, even though she recognized Émile's voice. He was wearing blue jeans, a green cotton shirt, and was carrying a bundle of brochures.

'Are you by yourself?'

Before she could answer he saw the others on the beach.

'I knew it,' he said.

48

'Knew what?'

'That they'd do this to you. They decided last night never to speak to you again and treat you as if you didn't exist.'

He remained standing, one hand resting on the arm of an unoccupied chair.

'Sit down for a moment.'

'No thanks. I don't want to disturb you and I'm not looking very smart. Marie-Lou tried to stick up for you.'

'Are you sure she did?'

'Yes. I heard her say: "It's not really her fault! She gets so unhappy ..."'

'Isn't the *patron* at the Monico?'

'Was it you who rang up just before four? I thought it might have been, but Madame Touzelli had already hung up. He's taken Madame Florence to Nice, to see a doctor.'

'Is she ill?'

'I don't know. He rang up a doctor I've never heard of and made an appointment ... You won't be angry, Mademoiselle Célita, will you, if I tell you ...'

He hesitated, abashed, turned towards the sea and went on:

'... If I tell you that I'm on your side?'

'You don't think I played a dirty trick?'

'That's not for me to say, is it? I know that as far as you're concerned I don't count, I'm just a kid, and what I think isn't important ...'

'What do you think?'

Down on the beach they were nudging each other, staring at the odd couple, Émile and Célita.

'You needn't be frightened! Tell me!' she went on.

'I don't think you were getting what you're after, with the boss, that is.'

'What am I after?'

'Madame Florence's place. Everybody knows that. She too.'

'Has she said anything to you about it?'

'I've heard her mention it to her husband.'

'What did she say to him?'

'You want me to tell you?'

'Yes.'

'... "If you suppose I'll ever let that whore take my place at the desk ..."'

'Did you believe her?'

He blushed without answering and there was a slightly awkward silence. But after a while he sighed, then murmured, still hesitating:

'If you ever need me for anything, I'll be there.'

'Do you think I ever will?'

'I know the boss. I was fifteen when I came to the club. He thinks he's a tough nut. He doesn't stick his neck out with Ludo though, because Ludo probably knows a bit too much about him. As for Madame Florence, she knows him better than anybody else; she gives him a bit of rope, but she realizes he'll always come back to her in the end. Can I ask you one question that's been on my mind?'

'Go ahead.'

'Do you love him?'

She looked at him, her eyes hard.

'Tell me you don't love him,' he went on, 'that he sometimes disgusts you.'

'All men disgust me.'

'Me too?'

'You're only a child.'

'You think that too, I know you do, and you don't see that I'm the only person who loves you. You sleep with the boss. You sleep with other men too. I'm not saying that to make you angry. Some of them have even told me details about it afterwards ...'

He spoke ardently, in a low voice.

'Why do you keep on treating me like a kid? Listen! Don't look at me like that. What's stopping you doing with me what you do with other people?'

She could only shrug her shoulders, amazed and angered at the same time.

'Is it such a big thing to ask you? And you see how happy it'd make me!'

'Who else have you been asking this sort of thing?'

He smiled, flattered, in spite of himself, and acknowledged:

'Some people don't have to be asked.'

'Who?'

'You'd be surprised if you knew.'

'Who?' she repeated.

'One of them's pretty near here.'

'Ketty?'

'I don't count Ketty, she does it with everybody.'

'Natasha?'

He nodded his head and Célita sat still, musing. It was quite possible after all. And thinking about it she even seemed to understand Natasha's reasons for wanting to seduce Émile.

'I swear it's different with you, Mademoiselle Célita. I only told you about that to prove I wasn't still a kid. I love you . . .'

She had to smile.

'It's true, honest it is; and if I had a proper job and didn't have military service still to do, I'd marry you like a shot. . . .'

'Thank you.'

'Why do you say it like that?'

'No reason, Émile. I really meant thank you.'

'Then, is it yes?'

'It's no.'

'But why?'

'There's no why about it. Now please leave me alone.'

Thereupon, disconcerted, but unable to give up hope, he stuttered:

'Not even for five minutes?'

'What do you mean?'

'Just for us to be alone somewhere for five minutes . . .'

He couldn't understand why she suddenly got up and walked away without saying a word. She was abandoning thus her sole ally, leaving him bewildered in the middle of the Croisette, a batch of pink leaflets in his hand.

He had naïvely asked her for five minutes!

She was prepared for what would happen, yet she determined none the less to go to Justin's for supper that evening as

51

usual, merely planning her entry a little late so she could be the last to arrive. Francine always had her meals with her little boy, but the four others were there, at the table at the back, and Maud was sitting in the place usually kept for Célita.

When she came in, Justin looked embarrassed.

'They said you weren't coming.'

'It doesn't matter, Justin. I'll eat here.'

It was Natasha who was directing operations, she felt sure of it, and Maud was obviously uncomfortable that Célita was sitting by herself at a table near the door.

No move was made towards her. To rile her, the four women were endeavouring to carry on an animated conversation, but it was proving difficult, there were many silences, and they looked like amateur actors putting on a play in the village hall.

'So I told the old boy what I thought of him . . .'

'The one with the little beard?'

'No, the other one, who comes with that woman with all the new dresses and always pretends to go to the toilet in the hope of catching me in the cloakroom . . .'

Ketty interrupted her:

'He tried it on me as well. He wanted to make a date with me.'

'I told him I was an artiste, and for the sort of thing he was after I could give him a good address . . .'

Did she look round at Célita on purpose? Was the glance meant to insinuate things?

'Whose address did you give him?'

'He didn't want it. In any case he didn't have time to listen to any more. He'd just seen his wife, through the peep-hole, coming across the floor, and he dashed off to the lavatory. . . .'

'Justin! Is there any strawberry tart?'

'It's all gone, Mademoiselle Natasha. But there's still some *mille-feuilles*.'

It was hard to eat without looking at them, hard too to look at them blankly enough, and the meal seemed to last an eternity to Célita. Finally, she kept her mind occupied by counting the cigarette butts in the sawdust on the floor below the bar, then the bottles on the shelves.

It was essential to stick it out, not only here, but later at the Monico where it would probably be worse. That afternoon on the beach they had had plenty of time to work each other up and plan all manner of spiteful things.

'Justin! Some Brie and a coffee, please!'

'Coming, mademoiselle.'

A newsvendor came in and she got through the rest of the meal by burying her head in a paper. She left last as she had intended, which entailed her being three minutes late, and from the doorway she saw Madame Florence taking the black notebook from the drawer.

'Good evening, Madame Florence.'

The *patronne* pointed to the alarm-clock on the shelf; Célita didn't give her time to speak.

'Yes, I know, five hundred francs.'

Ludo, overhearing this, opened his eyes wide; it was the first time he had ever heard anyone speak so cheekily to the *patronne*. Madame Florence was about to retort and call Célita back as she pushed open the door into the cloakroom, but in the end she simply marked a cross against her name, then, after a moment's hesitation, added another.

It was Saturday and the people were different; younger on the whole, they turned up earlier. Until half past ten nothing much happened, although they all continued to ignore Célita and exchanged knowing looks as if something were being hatched between them.

At half past ten the place was three-quarters full and almost everybody was dancing. Célita had been cornered by a dentist from Lille who had come to the Riviera to enjoy himself and was determined to enjoy himself at any cost. To be ready for the cabaret, about which he asked incessant questions, he had chosen a table on the very edge of the floor and in twenty minutes he had already finished his first bottle of champagne.

Unfortunately he was a keen dancer, and although he had obviously never been taught, he was convinced that his improvisations were irresistible. Every five minutes he went up to Gianini confidentially, and asked him to play one of his favourite tunes.

'One thing about you, you do let me do the leading,' he told Célita happily, as he made her perform the most fantastic steps. 'I hate women who think it's their job to show a man how to dance ...'

He didn't care if he jostled other couples or trod on his partner's toes, or that he almost fell over several times. On the contrary, the more violent the bumps the gayer he seemed, like somebody driving a dodgem car at a fair.

He felt down Célita's thighs and remarked:

'Funny to think I'll soon be seeing you without any clothes on, here on this very floor! How does it make you feel? Do you get excited?'

Still, every so often he had to sit down for a rest and, above all, a drink, and this gave Célita some respite.

It was while she was enjoying one of these respites that certain looks, smiles, attitudes made her feel that something was going to happen any moment now, but she found it in vain to imagine where the blow would fall. They were all there, almost all of them with a man, except Natasha and the new girl who were dancing together.

'Let's have another,' the dentist said, wiping his lips.

Since Madame Florence was watching her, Célita didn't dare refuse, and she was back on the floor again in the grip of her dishevelled partner. Had someone told the band to quicken the rumba rhythm? Gianini had been watching the dentist and probably thought he'd have a bit of fun.

Célita was following him as well as she could, bumped from left to right, and then all at once her leg twisted, for no apparent reason. She was on her knees before she realized that Natasha had danced past with the new girl and had deliberately hooked one of her high heels in such a way as to jerk off Célita's shoe.

Instinctively she tried to retrieve it, but she could not go on squatting between the dancers' legs and the shoe had already been kicked far away from her.

The dentist, who had no idea what was happening, asked her:

'Have you twisted your ankle?'

'No. It's my shoe. . . .'

Unable to dance with only one slipper, she attempted to leave the floor but had little success in pushing her way through the throng.

Three times, four times, she bent down to pick up her black suède shoe, already smudged with dust, whenever it came near her, and each time somebody sent it flying out of reach. It had developed into a game, a sort of football match everybody eventually joins in.

'Excuse me, please.'

She shoved several couples aside, made her way, limping, to her table, as people burst out laughing. Can one ever feel sorry for a woman who looks ridiculous?

'How did it happen?' her partner asked her, resignedly following her off the floor.

'It doesn't matter! Don't bother about me.'

Maud, who was still dancing with Natasha, was not laughing, nor did she try to kick the suède shoe, which had already lost a heel in the scrum. And Marie-Lou was the first to drop the game and take her partner over to the bar.

The music stopped. The floor emptied. Amongst the streamers in the middle lay the pathetic shoe, stared at by everyone until Jules decided to go and pick it up.

'Is this yours, Mademoiselle Célita?'

The question must have been ironical, when she was sitting there with one foot bare.

'I'll try and find the heel for you. It must be under one of the tables.'

'Don't worry, thanks, Jules.'

And her idiot dentist asked:

'I hope you've got another pair?'

'Upstairs, yes.'

It was better not to try and cross the room until the customers had started dancing again.

'Will you pour me a drink?'

She bravely managed to smile at him over her glass.

'Skin off your nose!'

Chapter 4

ALONE in the dressing-room, she collapsed on to a stool in front of the mirror and stared at herself, severely, without pity; probably, at that moment, she hated herself as much as the others hated her.

The grotesque incident of the shoe had shaken her more than if it had been something more serious, and if she had had even five thousand francs to her name she would have left the place that very minute.

She had no idea where she would have gone. She was too old for the Paris clubs. There was indeed a cabaret in Geneva which was a kind of Mecca for striptease artistes, where she had already been for two spells, but it was like a factory belt, fifteen girls every night, sometimes more, following one after another in a series of arranged items. Try Nice? Marseilles?

Still, what was the point of thinking about it when she didn't even have the train fare? She had never had any money, here less than ever, since as soon as she had her hands on a few notes she went and staked them at the Casino, not even at roulette or chemin de fer, for she had no ticket for the gaming-room, but at lotto in the big hall.

She would go back there the following week, however much she lost, as if to try to force her own fate into such a position that it would eventually have to play fair and make her win.

And while she was waiting for this to happen one day, she was more or less trapped in Cannes, with no chance of escaping; nor was it for the first time: she had been in a similar predicament in the past, in Ankara, an odd sort of place, a capital city built out of nothing, right in the middle of the Asia Minor desert.

She had blessed her good luck when she had been sent out there by a Porte Saint-Martin agency with a six-months contract, and never dreamt that the six months would turn out to be two years.

The cabaret had been a shabby affair, and right round the room there were private boxes which could be curtained off. In all her life she had never fought off so many hands. Each day she swore she would put some money aside for the journey back, whatever the cost, but after two years she was still there, towards the end almost resigned to the fact that she would be there for ever, which might have happened had it not been for a Belgian diplomat who was returning to Europe with his family and offered her the job of accompanying his children as their governess.

'You mustn't tell my wife where I met you. I'll pretend that you're a schoolmistress who wants to go home.'

During the journey he made the most of her, suggested keeping her with them at their home in Brussels, not very enthusiastically it is true, because although it was convenient for him, he was none the less terrified his wife would find out about their relationship.

She had those marvellous green eyes which change colour according to the weather, like the sea, and her hair was naturally dark auburn, she never had to tint it; and everybody told her with sickening repetition that her chin and her pointed nose reminded them of the young Colette, the Colette of *Claudine à Paris*.

Everybody considered her sexy. Just now, hadn't the dentist on the spree asked her about her act, which he had not yet seen:

'Doesn't it make you excited when you come out in front of everybody naked?'

He didn't know that she never appeared naked. And besides, if he'd had the opportunity to question them all, one after the other, he would have got a shock to learn that the girls from the Monico were less sexy than those on the beach for example, where Célita often watched women, young girls even, brazenly revealing themselves to all eyes, lying out flat on the warm, flesh-like sand, bringing themselves to a climax of excitement.

Maybe Maud was like that though; unless, as Célita suspected, she was simply putting it on last night.

As far as the others were concerned, men hardly aroused them at all. Marie-Lou, for example, sometimes got struck on somebody, but more like a teenager, almost like a little girl, and it was usually because, as she naïvely put it, 'he's such a sweet person'.

Natasha found she could sleep alone for weeks and months on end since she left her husband, and what had happened with Émile was something apart, a strange, unexpected pleasure she had allowed herself in passing, rather as one might treat oneself to some untried delicacy when travelling.

Francine lived for Pierrot and nobody else; she would have liked more children provided the father passed out of her life as soon as possible.

Ketty was the exception. She alone was aggressively and crudely sex-conscious, so that she spoke about making love in the dirtiest way, like some of the clients they tried to avoid, but Célita suspected that she exaggerated it all to hide the fact that she was frigid.

For Célita, Madame Florence and probably millions of other women as well, a man didn't mean sex, nor was it, at any rate not entirely, a question of security.

That afternoon Émile had asked her a question which kept running through Célita's head:

'*Do you love him?*'

He had added, naïvely, like the kid he was:

'*Doesn't he sometimes disgust you?*'

Well no, he didn't. And perhaps, in her own way, Célita was in love with Léon. Because she had chosen to conquer him. Because she had selected him as her adversary.

He was a match for her in fact, and since he was continually slipping out of her range, he made the contest difficult, and all the more exciting.

Madame Florence had been through it all too, probably, for she had remained faithful to him, working for him while he was in prison, and also now helped him day after day, showing him she was intelligent enough to ignore his weaknesses.

Célita had decided to take him from her, and it was neither

dastardly nor treasonable on her part. It was honest warfare.

Was she going to give up the struggle because of a shoe kicked off her foot, because of a ridiculous girls' conspiracy like a boarding-school conspiracy?

It was not true that she had a spare pair of shoes here, as she had told the dentist. The only shoes she kept at the Monico were some red satin ones, with rhinestones sewn on them, which she wore for her Spanish dances.

Downstairs they probably thought she was sulking, or crying, or getting her things together to leave. She trembled when she heard steps on the iron staircase, but did not glance through the glass pane down by the floor to see who was coming.

When the door opened she saw Léon's reflection in the mirror. He held a hammer in one hand, the retrieved heel in the other, and without saying anything he looked about for the shoe, picked it up, walked across to the window ledge.

He loved doing odd jobs, particularly difficult ones, and he turned the black suède shoe round and round in his big fingers for a long time before taking some nails from his pocket and setting to work.

The window ledge was unsuitable for what he wanted to do, so he looked about him again, finally noticed the stool Célita was sitting on.

Wasn't he paying her this visit to hold out the olive branch? He was absorbed in his task, frowning, biting his tongue, and he turned the stool upside down to mend the shoe on one of its legs, using it like a cobbler's last.

'Hold the toe.'

He had several goes before he was satisfied with the solidity of his handiwork.

'That'll hold for now, but you'd better not dance on it.'

She took the shoe from his hands.

'Thanks.'

'That's all right.'

At the door he spoke again, without turning round:

'You must admit you asked for it!'

When she came downstairs, shortly after him, Natasha had

59

taken her place at the dentist's table, and he looked at Célita in embarrassment but didn't invite her back. It would not be long before Marie-Lou and Ketty went up to change into their costumes, and as she walked towards the bar and hoisted herself on to a stool, Célita realized that Marie-Lou would not be sleeping at the Place du Commandant-Maria that night.

The last Saturday in every month, the 'Man from Switzerland', as they called him, not knowing his real name, would sit in a corner by himself, indifferent to what was going on about him: one evening, quite naturally, without realizing how odd his behaviour seemed, he had taken a newspaper from his pocket and started reading.

He was a bank manager from Geneva and each month he came to Cannes to see a rich customer who was ending his days in one of the most beautiful villas on the Riviera, which he never left except in a car, accompanied by his chauffeur and his nurse.

On his first visit to the Monico, the Swiss had watched them one by one and stayed till closing time. He had danced only once, solely to have the opportunity of speaking to Marie-Lou, who, with her innocent ways, inspired more confidence in him than did the others.

'I shan't be coming back with you tonight,' Marie-Lou had announced to Célita as they were getting dressed to go. 'That chap's waiting for me at the corner.'

They had been seen walking off towards the Croisette. Marie-Lou came home at seven o'clock the next morning, and, since she hadn't got her key, had knocked on the door for ages before she could wake Célita.

'I'm sorry, darling. Do you know what he did? He put his alarm on for six o'clock without telling me, and then informed me that I'd got to go and take care not to let the servants see me. He's staying at the Carlton, in a suite with an enormous drawing-room, number 301, I remember. We didn't even go inside together. He was scared of the porter and told me:

'"Go up to number 301 in ten minutes and don't speak to anybody."'

'He expected I'd be walking up and down the Croisette

while I waited. Of course I went and had a chat with Louis, the night-porter . . .'

Since then the same performance happened every month and the Swiss had never thought of changing his partner. He was satisfied with Marie-Lou, and as she herself said, he hated anything unexpected, anything that makes life complicated, insisted that everything should conform, once and for all, to established rites.

Because he was there this evening Célita almost changed her plans once again, for the idea of going home alone, particularly tonight, made her depressed. She couldn't leave Cannes without money, but nothing obliged her to stick to Léon, nothing prevented her from going for another man.

The person in the grey tweed suit, the one she had called 'God the Father', was here again, sitting in the same place as the night before, with his irritating smiling equanimity, and she was convinced it was to see her that he came. She obviously fascinated him. Had he witnessed the scene over the shoe?

Why shouldn't she join battle all over again, with him, starting from scratch?

She leant over to Ludo who had just poured her a whisky: 'Do you know who that is?'

He looked in the direction indicated, shook his head.

'I was wondering too. He doesn't come from Cannes, but he's French and drives a big convertible. Last week, when I was doing some extra work at the Yacht Club, he was there, with all the nobs.'

The man had guessed they were talking about him, and even what they were saying, because, joining in the game, he took a visiting-card from his gold-monogrammed wallet, called the barman and required him to give it to Célita:

She read:

COMTE HENRI DE DESPIERRES

There were two addresses, one on the left, the other on the right: on one side, 'Château de Despierres, par Péri-gueux'; on the other, '23 rue François-Ier, Paris'.

She walked over and gave him back his card, saying very coldly:

'Thank you.'

'May I buy you a drink?'

'Not now. I've just had a scotch, and I'd been drinking champagne before that. I'll have to go and get ready soon in any case.'

'I know the time-table.'

She saw Léon, near the door, watching them, and once again she was tempted to drop everything and start afresh.

'Are you staying on the Riviera long?'

'Until my wife decides she's had enough.'

She had already noticed the ring he wore on the third finger of his right hand, as well as the signet ring, on which she now realized his coat-of-arms was engraved.

'Disappointed?' he asked.

'Why?'

'You might have had ideas about me. If things start going wrong one way, it's only natural to try another.'

'What do you mean?'

He merely looked in the *patron*'s direction.

'Who told you about that?' she insisted.

'Nobody. I've got eyes. You're a strange girl, Célita.'

He had seen her name on the photos, in the front, but she was none the less disconcerted.

'Your friends are upstairs already. I thought you had to go and change. What are you doing tonight? The can-can?'

The whole time he seemed to be laughing at her, pleasantly, teasing her as an elder brother might, and that made her angry; she pursed her lips, left him without saying a word, and went up to the dressing-room.

The show was starting. Ketty was going on to the floor. Marie-Lou was finishing pulling on her black mesh tights and after hesitating a moment, because she had promised not to speak to Célita, she said quietly:

'This evening, I'm ...'

'I know, I saw him. ...'

Marie-Lou was not one for complications and now, as she was alone in the dressing-room with Célita, she found herself in a more difficult position than the rest of them.

'You know it wasn't me who ...'

'Don't upset yourself about me!'

'Maud didn't want to either. Even so ...'

'Ah!'

'I promise you. She felt lost here, in a new place, so she clung to Natasha, or rather Natasha got her claws into her, and the kid doesn't dare ...'

Madame Florence's voice called, from below:

'Marie-Lou!'

'Coming, madame!'

She pulled at her black satin dress, looked at herself one last time in the mirror and hurried downstairs. Célita, in her lawn knickers and brassière, was putting on her stockings when Maud and Natasha arrived in their turn. In the fanlight she watched them come through the cloakroom and saw Natasha's gesture as she pushed the new girl, who hesitated, towards the staircase.

They both knew she was alone upstairs. Did Maud suppose that Célita would make a scene or tear her eyes out like a cat? But quite the opposite was going to happen, for Célita had made up her mind.

She was going to stay. She refused to alter her objectives. Count What's-his-name downstairs didn't interest her in the slightest, in spite of his tweed suits, his two houses and the signet ring with his coat of arms.

Natasha was undressing completely, whereas Maud was only bothering to re-do her face and change her knickers beneath her tucked-up skirt.

Célita, now ready to go down, looked from one to the other of them, and faced the new girl.

'I'm sorry,' she said, in a clear voice which did not tremble, nor ask for favours. 'I know when I'm in the wrong and I realize I played a mean trick. I've been made to pay for it. I don't bear a grudge against anybody.'

Nobody could tell what was going on underneath this. Abashed, Maud Leroy sought for an answer and, after glancing at Natasha, she mumbled:

'I don't bear you any grudge either, mademoiselle.'

She hadn't got used yet to their customary informality.

'You may as well shake hands now,' Natasha interposed. 'There's no point in going on hurting each other.'

Maud's hand was soft, the tips of her fingers rough, like the hands of women who do a lot of sewing.

Natasha went on, still naked, holding her g-string in her hand:

'It was I who found the heel of your shoe and gave it to the *patron*. As for the dentist downstairs, nothing would please me better if you'd have him back. In any case he'll be so tight after the show they'll probably have to cart him out to a taxi.'

As Célita was going downstairs, Natasha called her back:

'Aren't you going to shake hands with me as well?'

'If you want to. . . .'

It was not peace, but an armistice. Or rather, to Célita's way of thinking, it was indisputably war, this time. Léon had put himself out to come and mend her shoe, seeming to attach no importance to it, precisely because it was important.

She had sized up the new girl. He would go back to Maud once, twice, perhaps more often. She had youth on her side. But might not her mere nineteen years prevent her understanding what he wanted?

Florence understood, so did Célita. Because both of them were real women. Like all males, Léon had the urge to dominate, to convince himself that he was carrying off a victory, that he was reducing a female to mercy.

That was what he was looking for when he made love in such a brutal, almost vicious way, a cruel flame shining in his eyes.

Célita was ready to struggle with him, a kind of endless struggle, in which she was never absolutely vanquished and the man continually had to prove his prowess.

'You're a little bitch!' he often told her, at the very moment when he should have been most satisfied with her.

He would ask her questions, staring into her eyes, their teeth almost touching.

'You do it on purpose, don't you? Tell me you do it on purpose!'

She said yes, to goad him.

'Do you hate me?' he asked.

'I'm not sure.'

This was true, since she had joined in the game herself in the end. He was the male. He was the enemy. Whatever happened she had to win.

It was no longer a matter of security as far as she was concerned, and she wasn't holding on to him simply because she was scared of the Prisunic or the pavement which might lie in wait for her.

Life had done its best to drown her; each time that she had got her head above water, at the price of a terrible effort, somebody or something had been there to push her under again.

It was for her own sake, for the image she had formed of herself, that it was absolutely necessary to win this particular game.

She hadn't enough time left to take part in many more. On each occasion the odds grew longer against her. She had been putting all she had into this one for six months, all her ardour, all her determination.

Florence was also playing her last card, even more desperately, since she was forty years old and was falling ill.

Each was defending what she considered her own property. Neither was asking for any pity.

The position was clear, was it not?

A while ago Célita had almost given in, just over a shoe, because she had felt humiliated. She wouldn't have left, since that was impossible, but she had envisaged throwing herself at that lousy 'God the Father', who was a Count into the bargain.

She felt angry with herself now for having been able to think of it, even for a moment.

Maud had shaken her by the hand. Her skin was pale, there were needle-pricks at the tips of her fingers, and one felt something about her body to be unfinished or not quite healthy. In a few minutes she would be walking out on to the floor again, white with fear, glueing her eyes on Gianini, who supported her with his music as effectively as if he were holding her by the shoulders.

Perhaps she was not quite so innocent as she appeared? She had been able to make her decision all by herself, at Bergerac, and she had set off into the unknown with hardly enough to live on for a week. She had paid the price at Marseilles, sleeping with a barkeeper whom even Léon seemed to consider a brute. She had not hesitated to steal a handbag and later, for the detective's benefit, she had known how to burst into tears in the most touching way.

As for the striptease part of it, which kept everybody breathless, Célita was becoming more and more convinced that it was a fake.

In any case she had made a mistake to get involved in the fight, to climb into the ring as it were, to come between Célita and Madame Florence.

She was the wrong weight.

'And now, ladies and gentlemen, we have pleasure in introducing to you Mademoiselle Célita, the famous Spanish dancer who has been acclaimed in the leading cabarets of Europe ...'

Her face at the peep-hole, she smiled sarcastically. Marie-Lou brushed past her, hurried towards the staircase, leaving behind her a strong smell of sweat.

In five minutes everyone would know that Célita had sued for peace.

That evening there was another skirmish, but one of a different sort. Just before, as if to prove Natasha's point, the dentist, who had been giving a solo performance on the dance-floor, wearing a cardboard cowboy's hat, had suddenly collapsed while hanging on to a table, which had thereupon overturned, together with the bucket, the bottle of champagne, and the glasses.

The *patron* had helped Ludo to get rid of him, Jules had tidied up the mess and the band had struck up a rumba, while Maud, who had received as much applause as on the night before, went and sat by herself in the corner, still the same shy little girl.

Célita had deliberately not rejoined the Count; she saw him pay for his drinks, then instead of collecting his things from the cloakroom, walk over and sit down beside the new girl.

Maud was obviously still observing the rules of the game, or at least pretending to observe them, because, knowing Célita had previously been with her new escort, she turned towards her with a questioning look, as if asking her permission.

'Go ahead, girl!'

At least that was the meaning behind Célita's dumb show. Strange to say, it was the *patron* who seemed displeased, or worried. Was he afraid Maud might be taken from him even before he had had time to make the most of her?

Marie-Lou, who had just learnt of the reconciliation, passed close to Célita, and whispered to her, touching her shoulder:

'You did the right thing!'

'Thanks!'

She probably thought her advice had borne fruit. Poor fat fool!

Somebody asked her to dance just as a considerable party entered, four couples in a group, probably straight from the gala night at the Casino, since they were in evening dress, and tables were pushed closer together to make room for them.

The Count was not dancing. Leaning towards Maud he was talking to her seriously, as if he were proffering her the advice of an older and more experienced man of the world. Had he shown her his visiting-card yet?

During a break between dances, as Célita was having a drink at the bar, Ludo said to her:

'I saw the name on the card. I know him now. I'd heard about him but I didn't know this was the one. He married an American twenty years older than him, and she makes his life a misery ...'

It was now Célita's turn to put on a 'God the Father' smile as she looked over at Maud's companion.

'You prostitute!' she couldn't help muttering to herself.

To think that she had almost taken him on!

She looked around for Léon, found him in conversation with a regular visitor, a shopkeeper from the rue d'Antibes who only came to the Monico when his wife was staying with her mother, at Grenoble. The *patron* gave Célita a wink across the crowded room, as if to say to her:

'Well done, my girl!'

He had heard that she had made her apology, but he was far from suspecting the reasons that had prompted her to do so.

It was a long evening, an exhausting one, mainly on account of the party in evening dress, who, as well as champagne, had ordered caviare; all the girls except Maud, who only had one possible number, were obliged to dance twice instead of once.

The party looked as though they would never get tired, and even at four o'clock there was no telling when they would go.

Léon still kept his eye on Maud and the Count. At one stage, when the latter went off to the lavatory, the *patron* made a point of being in the cloakroom in order to waylay him.

Naturally enough he didn't make a scene. Célita could see him through the peep-hole, jovial, but embarrassed.

She could almost swear he would be saying something of this kind:

'That girl's not like the rest, you know ... I'd be careful if I were you ...'

He was keen to stake his claim to her before anyone else stole a march on him. Who knows but he might not presently send his wife off home by herself while he saw Maud back to the Hôtel de la Poste?

'Idiot!'

He reminded her of Émile who, trembling, begged her for five minutes as if his life depended on it.

The 'Man from Switzerland' was getting impatient. Marie-Lou had asked Madame Florence if she might leave before closing-time, but to no avail. Upstairs there was a typewritten notice, next to the mirror, giving the 'House Rules', which dealt with every possible contingency, particularly that the artistes were required to stay until 4 a.m. at least, and in any case never to leave until the last customer had gone. It also covered things like fines, personal hygiene, and the prohibiting of 'throwing cotton-wool, etc., down the w.c.'.

Two hours ago Célita had considered the idea of escaping from this tiny world in which chance had deposited her.

She was finding herself more deeply involved than ever, but she was going to face it with defiance.

She could no longer risk defeat.

They did not always bother to change in the morning before they returned home. Especially when it was very late, they often went off in the dresses they wore between shows, and carried, over their arms, the clothes in which they had come.

Closing-time was like the end of classes at school. The musicians could be seen putting their instruments away in their cases, Jules and the barman went round collecting glasses and empty bottles, while Madame Florence made up little bundles of banknotes and slipped them into a big yellow envelope which she took away in a handbag almost as big as a cabinet minister's portfolio.

Léon saw to the lights, sniffing in the corners, treading on cigarette ends, for he was haunted by fear of a fire, and he was always the last to leave, locking the door before joining his wife in their car.

They said good-bye more or less all round, as the opportunity arose. Everyone had, as it were, to fend for himself.

'Are you going to Justin's?'

'No. I'm not hungry.'

'I could do with some spaghetti ...'

Marie-Lou met her 'Man from Switzerland' at the street corner and they went off arm-in-arm towards the Carlton like a regular couple. They could hear the sound of the sea, saw it becoming paler with approaching day. In the harbour some fishermen were starting the motor on their boat, and at the Forville market the farmers' wives were setting out their baskets and crates, while Justin busily served coffee and white wine.

Célita had not seen the Count leaving. Maud had remained until the end and there was just a chance that the *patron* might have accompanied her back.

She was walking alone, careful not to twist the heel which had been mended, and just as she was taking the short cut, by the footbridge over the railway, she heard steps behind her.

She was always frightened at night-time, and although the sky had begun to turn pale, it was still dark. Without turning round she walked more quickly, her ears alert, sensing that the unknown person behind her had also quickened his pace.

She was almost about to break into a run, her key already in her hand, so that she could get inside the door as quickly as possible, when a voice called:

'Célita!'

She stopped still, murmuring:

'Idiot!'

For it was Émile's voice. He had stayed to change in the cloakroom and was wearing his blue jeans and a sports shirt, and must have been shivering in them.

He ran the few yards still separating them while she waited for him.

'What is it?'

'Nothing . . . I saw Marie-Lou with her Man from Switzerland, and I thought you'd be going home alone. . . .'

They walked along side by side and Émile skipped now and then as he did when he was nipping from car to car to put his leaflets behind the windscreen-wipers.

'I thought you were going back to Le Cannet on your bike . . .'

His father had been killed during the war and he lived at Le Cannet with his mother, who was a charwoman.

'I don't have to . . .' he said, without further explanation.

One didn't have to be very smart, after his avowals that afternoon, to guess what he was hoping for, and Célita wondered what she was going to do. She wasn't the maternal type, like Marie-Lou, for example, who, though only twenty-five, treated all men, including her pompous bank-manager, like over-grown babies.

Nor was she curious for experience like Natasha, for whom the boy had been a sort of delicacy one enjoys between meals.

She found herself in an awkward situation, since she didn't want to hurt Émile's feelings and at the same time felt a little scared of him. At the Monico, although he was right on the bottom rung of the ladder, for that very reason people were careless when he was about; he noticed everything, heard everything, and was even the only one to go to Florence and Léon's flat sometimes.

Was he already convinced he would attain his object? At any rate he wasn't talking about it.

'I hear you've been very nice, Mademoiselle Célita.'

'Who told you that?'

'Everyone. I was glad, and I knew you would from the start. I even had a bet with Ludo.'

'You bet him I'd apologize?'

'I bet him you wouldn't have things in for them. You're different from the rest. Natasha's the one who planned the whole thing. You'd better watch her. The others aren't intelligent enough to be nasty. By the way, I found out about the doctor at Nice. It's Madame Florence who's ill.'

'How do you know?'

'Because he's a specialist in women's diseases.'

'A gynaecologist?'

'That's the word, yes. I saw it in the telephone book but I couldn't remember it.'

They came in sight of the square, where the greengrocer was taking down the shutters of her shop, and an Arab was sitting on a bench, asleep, his head resting in his bent arms. Francine's light was on.

'You left the window open when you came out,' Émile remarked.

He was right. When she had left the flat Célita had not been in the mood to think about shutting windows.

71

'You shouldn't do that, not on the ground floor. You never know who might have climbed in. . . .'

She looked at him, trying hard not to laugh, for she saw through his little game.

'You're afraid for me, I suppose?'

'What if that bloke on the bench had decided to have a sleep inside, or to burgle the place. . . .'

'But he didn't, did he?'

'He's not the only one.'

'And you think you'd better come in and make sure?'

A moment before, he was smiling too, as if enjoying juggling with his little speeches. But now she had her foot on the doorstep Émile's face suddenly clouded over, he was so upset that he looked as if he would burst into sobs.

'Please, Mademoiselle Célita, I implore you . . .'

She wanted to say no, and she could not bring herself to do so. Not long ago Léon had looked at Maud with almost the same imploring expression and now she would have sworn that he had not had the patience to wait until the next day, that he had gone to the Hôtel de la Poste even if it did mean a row with Madame Florence.

She stayed there, hesitating, her hand holding the key she had already inserted in the lock.

'I'll leave as soon as you say . . . And if . . .'

He was loath to make this promise, but finally decided it was better than nothing at all.

'. . . And if you don't want me to, I won't touch you . . .'

She opened the door, pushed the light button, leaving the door open behind her. He closed it and she turned right in the passage, feeling him trembling all over behind her back.

With the second key she opened the door of the flat, remembering how untidy she had left it, with the beds unmade.

She realized, bitterly, that it was too late to go back on her decision.

'Poor Émile,' she said, turning on the lights. 'I think you'll be disappointed; you see how women live when they're left to themselves.'

A kind of fury stirred in her breast, and she shoved open

the bathroom door, to reveal the unemptied bath, the towels lying on the floor.

'Look . . .'

She switched on the light in the dining-room; the breakfast things had not been cleared from the table and the cups had dregs of coffee settled at the bottom.

'And here . . .'

The two unmade beds, the rumpled sheets, the greyish pillows at one end with traces of lipstick on them, and knickers soaking in the washbasin. . . .

'You still want to stay?'

She threw her coat over a chair, kicked off her shoes and, as she stroked her bruised foot, the poor booby declared, as if he were reciting the Hail Mary:

'I love you!'

Chapter 5

At the beginning of the evening they were all misled into thinking things were well again, including Célita, except perhaps that Célita did not dare to be hopeful too soon, being used to fate going against her. She had been to Justin's with Marie-Lou, and they had found Natasha and Ketty already sitting down to eat; as there were only two empty places at the table, Célita had paused for a moment, imagining that one of the two places was for Maud.

'I don't think she'll be coming,' Natasha had said to her. 'That's why I told them only to set four places.'

Something had happened, you could see from the excited look on their faces. Natasha continued:

'I rang up her hotel twice and both times they told me she was out. I called there on my way here. The proprietress told me that Maud had gone out at lunchtime without leaving a message, or having any breakfast, and she hasn't been back.'

At half past nine the four of them trooped into the Monico, like a line of schoolgirls almost, and each of them said good evening to Madame Florence; Célita thought she was looking drawn. At twenty-five to ten, as they sat in the dressing-room getting ready, Marie-Lou looked at her watch and murmured:

'Five hundred francs!'

A little later they were downstairs, at separate tables; they were told to do this in order to make the room seem 'furnished'. Madame Florence's eyes had dark rings under them and she had that anxious look of people who appear to be expecting an agonizing pain at any moment, so that Célita remembered her visit to the gynaecologist at Nice.

For a moment she had imagined that the *patronne* might perhaps be pregnant, but it was unlikely to happen now, at forty years old, for the first time.

It must be some disease of the womb since she had consulted a specialist. Half the women Célita had met had had some kind of operation, usually the removal of one ovary, sometimes of both, and it frightened her; the word 'womb' conjured up something mysterious to her, something almost sinister, and the thing she feared most in all the world was to see herself, one day, with a violet scar on her stomach.

Monsieur Léon, standing at the door, must have been aware of Maud's absence. He must also have noticed the looks the women were exchanging from each corner of the room, and twice he went through the curtain to stand with Émile on the pavement outside.

A quarter to ten ... Ten to ten ... Across the room Marie-Lou mouthed the words:

'A thousand francs!'

Célita had noticed that the *patron* had shaved with more care than usual, that there was still some talcum powder near his ear and that he was wearing a loud tie she had not seen before. Had he not looked worried, and if Maud had been there, she would have known for certain that he had gone to see her and got what he was after.

She was way off the mark, as she wasn't long in realizing. A couple had just come in, regular customers who always chose a place near the band. They were a husband and wife who, although both only in their middle fifties, had none the less been nicknamed Philemon and Baucis, since throughout the evening they would be holding hands, smiling at the show, smiling at each other, saying only a few words from time to time, like a very old married couple who knew they always thought the same thoughts.

Gianini was playing an old-fashioned waltz for them, popular thirty years ago, which they had requested the first time they had come and which must have brought happy memories back to them.

Léon went up to the till, leant over to whisper something to his wife. His face was more flushed than usual, as if he had caught a touch of the sun. Madame Florence shrugged her shoulders, with a resigned air, and he hurried outside like a man with a mission to accomplish.

Indeed he did have one. Célita would get all the details

75

later, bit by bit, from Émile, or from Ludo, who could hear from his place what they were saying at the cash-desk.

The Hôtel de la Poste was a few yards away, in the same street, and that was where Léon was running.

When he came back a quarter of an hour later he was alone, but his face was lit up and he was obviously finding it difficult not to look triumphant as he told his wife what had happened.

Maud had not arrived on time because she had gone to sleep after coming back from the islands, at seven that evening, and there had been nobody to wake her.

'Poor child!' Célita had sneered, when she heard the whole story from Émile, having gone out for a moment, against the rules.

As for the *patron*, he was behaving so like a love-sick swain that it was becoming embarrassing. It was out of character for him to lose control of himself like this and everyone had noticed his loud tie and the boyish almost frisky manner he was unintentionally adopting.

Did he realize he was making a fool of himself? He imagined he had set his 'mark' on the new girl, as he would put it, when in fact it was she who had set her mark so oddly on him.

He stood there, waiting for her impatiently, moved by the fact that he had found her asleep, unaware of the time, just like a child! Had she too caught a touch of the sun?

The business had not taken place in the drab hotel bedroom, for that would not have been romantic enough. He had gone with her by boat to the Îles de Lérins, like the honeymoon couples, and no doubt Maud had romantically let her hand trail in the water flowing by the side of the boat.

Had they climbed the uneven steps to the fortress, hand in hand, and visited the cell of the Man in the Iron Mask? Had they been to see the monks at Saint-Honorat afterwards?

Célita and Florence, both probably occupied with the same thoughts, did not dare look at each other now, they were so ashamed for him. It was not a touching sight, since he was long past Émile's age, but just ridiculous.

The silly ass was looking at his watch every couple of

minutes, unsuspecting that even the members of the band were exchanging winks.

Ketty was dealing with four new clients, Natasha and Marie-Lou were dancing together, when the new girl finally appeared, in the same little black dress she had worn the previous evenings, and half-opened the curtains with the hesitating, timid look of a mouse.

She went straight up to Madame Florence. Célita could not hear what she was saying, but she saw the *patronne*'s cold, resigned face as she dryly accepted the explanation – there was little else she could do – and directed her to her place at the front of the room.

Célita had under-estimated the girl from Bergerac; she realized that now. Maud Leroy had chosen the fragile approach: the 'poor little thing who is scared of life and needs a man's support'.

Léon, despite his experience of all sorts, had fallen for it! Even his walk had changed, had become lighter, more elastic. So youthful did he now imagine himself again that it seemed he might at any moment start jumping over the chairs, like people leaving the cinema who fancy themselves as the hero of the film.

He avoided catching Célita's eye, or his wife's. Had the latter already been warned of his new idea, which he was about to see realized? A reporter from the *Nice-Matin*, Julien Bia, who sometimes called at the Monico for a drink, came in, and this evening he had his camera with him. It was obvious that it had been arranged for him to come, that Léon had either called to see him or telephoned to him.

Sure enough, the *patron* rushed up to him, led him off to Maud's table, called Jules to order a bottle of champagne and three glasses.

He was determined to launch the kid, to make her into a star, and the journalist, who had interviewed most of the visiting celebrities along the Riviera, none the less gravely took a pen and pad from his pocket and dutifully prepared to take notes.

He asked her questions as if she were somebody really

important, jotted down her answers, and the little slut played her role so well that Célita had a furious desire to walk over and slap her face.

Her sweet-little-girl look was too good to be true, shy and sulky at the same time. Trust Léon, the former pimp, not to make the mistake of buying her a new dress and giving her a hair-do and a manicure!

She was quite capable of having thought of that for herself. She still managed to appear the sort of kid one might meet in the street or behind a counter, or, better still, the young girl who has just stepped off an all-night train, slightly rumpled, tired-looking, holding a cheap suitcase, and you don't know where she's come from, nor where she's going.

Nor would she have changed her underclothes, nor her stockings; she was too clever for that. Her cheap little pants, like those worn by typists and skivvies, stimulated men's imagination and gave them a greater impression of feminine mystery than the mesh tights, black wasp-waists, and spangled g-strings the professional girls wore.

What could she be telling the reporter in her artless way, as if her adventure was the most ordinary thing in the world, as if all the small-town girls of France were leaving home to start taking their clothes off in night clubs the very next day?

It would be in the paper tomorrow. Not everything, since more than fifteen minutes had gone by, enough time for the reporter to fill two columns with her story, before he put away his pen and paper in his pocket.

He got up, stepped backwards to take the photographs, while Léon modestly moved a little apart from her along the bench and Madame Florence turned her head away.

Julien Bia was not leaving yet. He waited until Maud's number was over, because he also had to have some shots of the girl in action. He even took one of her almost naked as she leaned over backwards on the floor, in a sort of spasm, but this one would certainly never appear in the newspaper. It was for Léon!

Gianini had changed his compère's patter, and it was obviously not he who had composed the new formula.

'And now, ladies and gentlemen, the management of the Monico have the honour and the pleasure of presenting to you the great discovery of the year, the artiste who will be tomorrow's unrivalled queen of striptease, Mademoiselle Maud Le Roy, nineteen years old, who has astounded, and will continue to astound, everyone who has seen her ...'

The management had the *honour* ...

The name Le Roy they had split into two words and it would appear as such in the paper the next morning, not only in the account of the interview, but in the large advertisements which would announce Maud to the public in letters four times the size of those of the other dancers.

And besides this, outside the club and on the walls of the town, a band was to be pasted across the old notices until new ones should be ready:

Mademoiselle Maud Le Roy
The year's most exciting sensation

Célita and Florence were not the only ones to have realized all this and to be acting accordingly. As the evening wore on, the others also became glummer, as if the new girl had just taken something away from them.

The atmosphere was different. Granted, whenever a new artiste had arrived, there had always been a certain tense curiosity, and in a way they formed common cause against the stranger as they waited to see whether she would last, and whether she would prove a good sort or not.

Nor was it the first time the *patron* had taken a personal interest in a dancer, but at least he had remained himself, and more often than not it had been the girl who won sympathy.

This time a new element had entered into the Monico and Célita had been alone in sensing the danger right from the first day.

'It's time, Marie-Lou. .... Tell Ketty ...'

'Yes, madame.'

Madame Florence was not so bad-tempered, not so much the *patronne*, and all at once they wanted to be nice to her.

Occasionally Léon had to sit with some of the clients, or buy a detective or a journalist a drink or a bottle of wine. He had never been known to remain sitting there like this, for two hours, indifferent to the thousand details on which he normally kept an eye.

Contrary to what one might have expected, they hardly mentioned it when they were upstairs changing, or when they passed each other on the iron staircase or in the cloakroom. Nor did they exchange the facile little jokes which the situation might have provoked.

It was rather like an illness weighing upon them all, perhaps because they realized that the situation was out of their control, and there was also a degree of embarrassment in addition to their natural uneasiness.

Would one of them be kicked out now there was another permanent number in the show? Ketty was the least successful performer, who was usually sent on first when people had not quite settled into their seats. But Ketty had been there the longest. As a hostess, she had more go than the others. And lastly – but it was never mentioned – she was ready to follow any client back to his hotel, after the show, or arrange to meet him the next day.

Was Marie-Lou perhaps in a more dangerous position since it was impossible to get her to wash herself properly and send her clothes to be cleaned, in spite of fines and Madame Florence's continued admonitions?

Her good temper stood her in favour; she was the only one who never had her bad days, and she coped equally well with rowdy drunks and the kind of client who wanted to tell his life story.

Natasha's sculptural nakedness was the photo in the glass show-case which attracted the most people. And up till now Célita's had been the 'prestige' number. She was a real dancer, the only one. In other words, the Monico was not a vulgar dive where one only went to watch girls undressing, it was an artistic cabaret.

'I'll be the one!' she announced to Marie-Lou whom she found deep in thought by the cloakroom door.

They were obviously all preoccupied by the same subject, for Marie-Lou simply replied:

'More likely me!'

They had been sharing a secret all day. Marie-Lou had come home early, because her Swiss friend, scared of the servants as usual, had made her get up at six o'clock. She had spent a good ten minutes in the bathroom before going back to bed, for she had had three abortions and the last had almost finished her off, so that now she took double precautions.

Célita had vaguely heard her getting into bed; then, later the alarm had sounded, Marie-Lou had gone to make the coffee, and when she had set the table and there was a semblance of order in the dining-room, she had come and pulled off the sheet Célita had twisted around her.

'Get up, lazybones!' she had called, good-humouredly, although normally she would never open her mouth before she had drunk her coffee.

Célita had finally opened her eyes and had then realized. Marie-Lou, with her floral wrap open, revealing her big breasts and the black triangle below her stomach, was wearing Émile's cap on her head.

'Well, my little slut! . . .'

What could Célita say? She didn't regret what she had done. In all her life she had never seen a person's face show such happiness as Émile's had done last night, and on leaving he had awkwardly kissed her two hands and mumbled:

'Thank you! I'm sorry. . . .'

'Sorry about what?'

Then he said something she had not expected, which she was to recall many times afterwards:

'For only being me!'

He was a good boy! That evening when she had come into the Monico with the others, he had had the tact, so uncommon among men, not to stare at her in any special way, but to act as if nothing had happened between them.

Marie-Lou had been nice about it too, in the end. She had not teased her too much. And almost immediately she had become serious and promised:

'Don't worry. I won't breathe a word.'

She had told her how she had lain with the boy one afternoon, almost by accident, when she had been to the Monico
to fetch her dress, and the *patron* had been out. They had
done it in the cloakroom among the bottles and party hats,
while the two old women were sweeping up the paper
streamers on the other side of the peep-hole.

Marie-Lou realized that it meant more to Célita than it had
to her. There was at least one quality one was bound to grant
her: humility. She placed herself on the bottommost rung of
the ladder, seeing herself as a household drudge who had
preferred to earn her living by taking off her clothes in public
than by drying dishes and washing floors.

Natasha impressed her because she read serious books and
because you could tell she'd had some education. In her
eyes, Célita was even better. She not only had a famous father,
but she was a real dancer, who had appeared in the big
theatres in Paris.

Ketty came of peasant stock too and had spent her youth
in a poverty-stricken village in Savoy. But as she was so fond
of asserting, she was an egalitarian and no one could impress
her, neither the rich nor the well-educated, although she did
have an unconscious passion for doctors, perhaps because
she contrasted them with the priests, for whom her Catholic
childhood had left her with nothing but hatred.

It was half past twelve when the journalist left, escorted
right to the door by the *patron*, who stayed a few minutes
longer with him on the pavement outside. When Léon came
back, he went straight over to the till, a little humiliated to
have to go and explain things to his wife, and he had hardly
begun talking to her before he was frowning at the sight of
an American officer in mufti sitting down at Maud's table
and engaging her in conversation.

Through Ludo, Célita later learnt what Léon had said to
Madame Florence:

'Julien Bia is of my opinion. He thinks she's terrific and
says I should sign her up, with a long contract.'

Madame Florence had replied:

'Most of them are terrific the first few days.'

That was true. More precisely, it was either all or nothing. They were either flops, overcome by panic, or their very shyness, the excitement they felt as they faced the public, communicated itself to the audience, won the day for them.

It wasn't till later when they tried to perfect a proper number that difficulties began, and so few of them were able to surmount them that cabaret proprietors were always at a loss how to reinvigorate their programmes.

But how could Léon be anything but optimistic after his excursion to the islands?

'She's caught on. She's a much more intelligent girl than I thought. Her nervousness is deceptive. You know what she said to Bia?

'"You've got to try and make the spectators feel they're surprising a woman in her bedroom, not watching an artiste do an act. . . ."

'She added:

'"Since I'm no artiste and haven't had any experience, it won't be difficult for me."

'"Unless you find you can't help getting experienced," our friend Bia retorted, the wise guy.

'And she said:

'"I'll take care to stay just as I am, not to change my way of life or my ideas."'

It was half past one when Ludo had reported this conversation to Célita, and the *patronne*, who had been feeling, or pretending to feel, unwell all evening, had gone home to bed, a rare thing for her, and left the cabaret in her husband's care.

Célita had wondered whether this was a strategic withdrawal, a rather naïve way of making an impression on Léon, yet it was true that Madame Florence had not been in good health for some time, and she had been to consult a gynaecologist.

The Maud affair had gone further than they could have foreseen, and it was impossible, as yet, to say which of them, she herself or Léon, had had the idea that showed near-genius.

This too emerged from the conversation between Léon and his wife immediately after the departure of the journalist. For Maud had said to the latter:

'I'll take care to stay just as I am, not to change my way of life or my ideas.'

Whereupon Julien Bia had objected, looking around him rather ironically:

'You'll have a hard job if you spend all your evenings here.'

And, raising his glass:

'And if you start drinking champagne and whisky with the clients!'

Was it not a stroke of genius on Maud's part to have answered:

'That's exactly why I'm going to ask Madame Florence not to let that happen to me. It's in her interest as well as mine. Sitting here at a table or at the bar I'm no use, I'm not a hostess. And if the clients see me here doing that sort of job, they'll stop believing in my act. Don't you see! I must stay looking like the girl next door.'

She must have slid the *patron* a conspiratorial glance, as she said this. Either he had thought up this idea, or it was she, and, if so, she was formidable.

How could the fool's conceit of himself as a potent male fail to be flattered by her wanting to keep out of other men's touch? What exactly had passed between them on the island? Célita was tempted to believe nothing had happened at all. Maud had probably pretended to be the poor little girl whose two experiences of sex – no, three, since there was the Marseilles episode – had left her wounded, feeling unclean, needing time to forget, needing patience, tenderness.

'Smart work!' Célita couldn't help saying to Ludo.

'You smelt a rat from the start! I'm beginning to wonder if it mightn't have been better for all concerned if Inspector Moselli had hauled her off without further ado.'

'What did Madame Florence reply?'

'They've made no decision yet. The *patronne* did her bit. Besides, that's when she mentioned the pains in her stomach and announced that she didn't think she'd be able to last out until closing time.'

That was quite smart work too, since there are occasions when one should know how to beat a retreat. That evening she was an obstacle, sitting there at the cash-desk, and her husband couldn't help feeling that she was spying on him – and hating her for it. Don't men need to imagine that they are free?

Her indisposition, whatever it was, came just in time, and after the second show Maud did not return to sit at her table. She descended the iron staircase wearing her hat, carrying a handbag, like a visitor, and Léon escorted her to the door, and then out on to the pavement.

He did not, however, go into her hotel but returned straight away looking worried, and went behind the bar, where he unhooked the telephone receiver to call his flat.

'Is that you? ...' he asked in a low voice. 'How are you feeling? ... Have you switched on the electric pad? ... Nothing special here, no ... Wait a sec ... there are still ...'

His eyes swept the room.

'Still about twenty clients. We'll be shutting early ...'

She asked no questions about Maud, and in the end it was he who felt it necessary to add, as if reassuring her:

'I've sent the little one home to bed. She could hardly stand upright.'

'A double scotch, Ludo,' Célita called out loudly.

'Do you think you should, mademoiselle?'

She nodded her head. She felt miserable. It was not so much sadness as discouragement, sickness at heart. It made her furious to watch a man like Léon, who thought himself a real male, whom she had taken for a real male, in such a state over a little go-getter.

Once again, she felt she was not being treated fairly.

For the way Léon was behaving today was the way she would have wanted him to behave, though a little differently, with more dignity, *over her*.

She knew she was a real woman, a real female to match him, and he would never have made such a fool of himself by falling in love with her, as he had now, almost to the point of losing all perspective and dignity.

It was part of the game. It was to be expected. They would have made – they had already begun to make – a fine couple, passionate, tearing away from each other only to come together more completely, shattering one another's pride, humbling each other.

He had understood her so well that he had occasionally felt frightened of her, frightened of being dragged down into the abyss where she was making him want to remain engulfed with her.

Had Célita's hatred of Madame Florence become less bitter? She knew this was not so. She was sure of herself. She had only needed a little more time to detach him from a tiresome and ageing woman.

What could be wrong in that? They were the wild beasts, the three of them, and wild beasts make their own laws.

'May the best one win!' is the sporting phrase.

She was convinced she was the best.

He had never looked such a numbskull as he did that evening, with his air of sudden rejuvenation and embarrassment at his happiness. He didn't know what to do with himself, where to look. Deep down, he already missed his wife, or rather her reassuring presence at the cash-desk.

He couldn't fail to notice that everyone at the Monico, the entire staff, was glancing at him furtively, then exchanging woebegone looks with each other, even including Jules, the bald waiter, with the watery eyes of a spaniel.

'I'm fed up, Ludo!' she declared, emptying her glass.

'Take a sleeping tablet as soon as you get home, and you'll feel better tomorrow.'

She looked the *patron* up and down, and said sarcastically: 'Tomorrow? You think so?'

Léon heard her order another double scotch, knowing very well that she had just finished one and had had several drinks with clients. Would he say something to her, to stop her drinking, or would he tell Ludo not to serve her any more?

She looked straight at him, on purpose, trying to provoke

some sort of reaction, even to the extent of having a public showdown, here and now, right away; she was feeling ready to explode.

He preferred to pretend he had noticed nothing, to push open the door to the cloakroom and come back with some paper hats which it was unusual to distribute at so late an hour, since the customers no longer needed them.

'See that?'

'You'd better be careful, Mademoiselle Célita. When I was a lad I had a job in the Vincennes Zoo and at certain times of the year we weren't allowed to go in the cages of the male animals, even to clean them. It didn't stop them, a fortnight or three weeks later, being as quiet as lambs, quieter than ever, as if they were trying to make up for the way they had behaved.'

It didn't make her laugh. Natasha, whose partner had just left, came up to her and glanced at her watch.

'A whole hour to go! God, how my feet hurt!'

'It's not my feet,' Célita answered, 'it's my nerves, and I've decided to get tight.'

'You think that'll help?'

'Have you heard the latest?'

'What latest? So much seems to be happening these days!'

The night before, they would willingly have jumped at each other's throats, and now they found themselves on the same side, albeit with different reactions. With a trace of resentment in her voice, Célita began:

'Your protégée ...'

She stopped.

'I'm sorry.'

'Carry on. It's been a long time since I had a protégée. We have enough to do looking out for ourselves. Do you mean Maud?'

'She'll be hitting the headlines tomorrow.'

'So I've heard.'

'That's not all: she's only going to come down here for her number.'

Incredulous, Natasha turned to Ludo, who nodded in confirmation.

'That beats the lot.'

'You feel the same?'

'It won't affect me much. If they decide to sack me, I've always got a job to go to in Geneva. As for you, you'd better keep off the drink, or you'll make a fool of yourself in a minute.'

She didn't need to watch her long to see that. It was true. Célita's nerves were so tense that she needed something to make her relax, a scene, a fight, anything violent which could serve as an outlet for her pent-up fury, which was choking her.

'Why don't you report sick too and go home to bed? Take a couple of gardenal tablets. . . .'

Ludo's advice again!

Célita was sorry the Count wasn't there; she could easily have picked a quarrel with him. He irritated her enough to be a good pressure valve.

After distributing a few hats, Léon went and smoked a cigarette in the street with Émile, a thing he often did towards the end of the evening.

Célita was still bent on making some sort of a scandal and she went so far as to look around for a suitable victim among the clients, but there were only two couples left in the room and they were engrossed in each other.

She felt like going out into the street, without her coat, walking past the *patron*, along to the Hôtel de la Poste, and knocking on Maud's door.

'Open up, you little bitch!'

She would be forced to get out of bed and open the door, or Célita would make a terrible din on the landing.

'Now go back inside. Shut the door. Let's get it over with . . .'

Would Maud dare to put on her 'poor little thing' act and flutter her eyelashes over her falsely innocent eyes?

Célita wanted to use her hands, her nails on the soft, over-white skin. She needed to hurt, to make her cry out, make her beg for pardon.

'Now have you got it into your head that he's not for you? Answer me, girl! Answer me, you pathetic whore! Answer me, I tell you!'

She put her hand to her brow, looked across at Ludo, who shook his head, thinking she wanted another drink.

'Do you know her address at Bergerac?'

'I only know that her mother's a postwoman there.'

'Is her name really Leroy?'

She was forgetting the scene she had witnessed through the peep-hole, when the new girl had held out her identity card to Léon and he had read out her surname, half-aloud. If she couldn't go and fight it out with her in the Hôtel de la Poste, there was still another way of getting even.

When she left with Marie-Lou, half an hour later, Marie-Lou exclaimed:

'Where are we going?'

'To the post office.'

One of the counters was open all night. On a form she wrote out, with a scratchy pen:

'Madame Leroy, Post Office, Bergerac, Dordogne.'

Then, after pondering a moment, beneath the address:

'Your daughter Maud performing in striptease show at Monico in Cannes.'

'Signature?' the counter-clerk asked, after reading it without any reaction.

She added the first name that came into her head: 'Caroline Dubois', and there were no further questions.

Marie-Lou had been waiting discreetly at the door.

'You're sure you've not gone and done something silly?'

She laughed:

'It doesn't matter a hoot what I do at this stage! ... You don't feel like getting tight?'

'No. If you're going drinking, I'm going home.'

It was not really drink Célita wanted: she just wanted something to happen; it was more like some vague, unsatisfied need.

She undressed without talking, in the bedroom which

89

seemed gloomier than ever, more impersonal, plainly utilitarian in a way that wasn't even aggressively ugly.

Contrary to habit she went to bed naked, without cleaning her teeth, and it was Marie-Lou who got into bed last and turned off the light.

'Good night.'

'Good night.'

Minutes went past and by now Célita was aware what it was for which she had this almost painful longing: for a man, any kind of man as long as he would knock her down, hurt her, and shatter her nerves.

Perhaps it was because she had drunk too much and a kind of dislodgement was taking place in her mind, which was numbed between sleeping and waking, but she suddenly felt she had to get up, put on her coat, nothing else, and go and look for the first man she met in the street and ask him to relieve her need.

The night before, when she hadn't wanted it, Émile had been there.

Below, through the half-open window and the closed shutters, she could hear steps, bicycles passing, men going home from night-work or starting out for their day's jobs.

Her eyes open in the darkness, her body taut, her nipples hurting, she clenched her teeth, grinding their enamel, and a long time afterwards Marie-Lou's sleepy voice enquired from the next bed:

'What's wrong?'

In answer, shouting:

'Nothing! Do you hear? There's nothing wrong with me! I'm ...'

And suddenly relaxed, empty, she burst into loud sobs.

PART TWO

Chapter 1

EACH of her own accord, the three of them had chosen from their wardrobes their simplest, least conspicuous dress, and they had put on hardly any make-up; there in the garden, conscious of being observed, they seemed to be imitating the gestures and attitudes of girls on their way out from High Mass.

Natasha, having arrived first, had waited for the others in the steep, narrow street where Monsier Léon's old Pontiac was parked behind a long, low-slung sports-car, bright red, which belonged to the surgeon.

When her friends looked questioningly at her, Natasha had said:

'It began a quarter of an hour ago. Apparently we can wait in the garden, and anyhow, unless something goes wrong, we shan't find out much this morning.'

They were at the Estérel Clinic, in a quiet, old part of the town, where only cats and dogs were wandering along the streets, sectioned into blocks of shade and sunlight, and the people from a wineshop opposite were washing out bottles.

The garden, with its pale gravel paths, was shaded by trees, the foliage of each a different green, and near the wall at the back some hens were clucking behind a trellis fence.

It was unusual for them to be out of doors at such an early hour, all together too, for it was little more than half-way through the morning and they had had hardly any sleep. Most of the windows in the clinic were wide open and the patients, men and women wearing cotton dressing-gowns with thin blue stripes, came and stared at them one after the other.

Of the three, Célita was the palest and the most anguished. During the ten days Madame Florence had spent under observation, undergoing repeated examinations, X-rays, analyses, she had come almost every afternoon at visiting hours, and the place was now familiar to her.

She knew that the ground floor was reserved for maternity cases, and she had been in the corridor two days ago just when a woman in Ward 6 was being brought back, accompanied by a nurse with a bloodstained apron, who was carrying a baby.

The curtain at the window occasionally swelled out with the breeze, and, when it blew to one side, revealed the bed, the mother, motionless and relaxed, some white carnations on the bedside table and, further inside, the child's enamelled cradle.

Directly above Ward 6, the window-panes were of frosted glass, and behind those windows they were operating on the *patronne*.

Natasha was also feeling a little queasy.

'Apparently, at the last moment, when they came to take her away on the stretcher, she sat up in bed screaming that she wouldn't go through with it, she'd changed her mind, she'd sooner die in peace, and she made such a struggle that they had to give her two injections.'

The sky was blue, the air warm and still; birds were chirping in the trees, and a blackbird, completely unafraid, was hopping about the lawn, spying with a mischievous eye on the three girls.

'Where is he?' Célita asked.

'I think there's a waiting-room for relatives upstairs, next door to the operating theatre. I didn't see him. His car was already here when I arrived.'

They heard footsteps on the gravel, then saw Francine, who had walked up quickly, wearing her blue suit, a white hat on her blonde hair.

'It's Thursday,' she explained, 'and I couldn't find anybody to look after Pierrot, as he isn't going to school. I couldn't bring him along here either.'

'What did you do about it?'

'He's playing in the street; there aren't many cars about,

94

and the woman in the dairy said she'd keep an eye on him through the shop-window.'

She, in turn, looked up at the window with the frosted panes.

'Well?'

She realized nobody had any news, that they would just have to wait. After a while she asked Natasha:

'Have you heard from Ketty?'

'No. But someone saw her in Nice. That's the third person who's told me that, so it must be true. . . .'

Ketty, to everybody's surprise, had been Maud's first victim; it happened before Madame Florence entered the clinic, while she still sat behind the till at the Monico, for part of the night at least. Hadn't the *patronne*, even then, given up hope? She was obviously seriously ill, and it had been all the more upsetting in that it had happened so suddenly and had coincided with the business of Maud.

Célita, for one, was aware that the suddenness had only been apparent; Florence had admitted as much to her, from her hospital bed.

'I've been expecting something to happen for a long time,' she had confided in a gloomy voice. 'That's why I used to refuse to see the doctor. I've practically always had something the matter with me inside, and I haven't been able to bear having any relations with Léon for months, it hurts me so much.'

In less than two weeks she had become not only a sick woman, but exhausted, ageless, pitiable, her skin loose, her eyes grown too large and feverish, staring at you as if they sought the answer to some terrifying question.

'They won't tell me what's wrong with me, but with all the tests they've been taking I know it's a cancer and I'll never get out of this bed again. . . . Poor Léon!'

She was sorry for him. She bore him no ill will, only regretted that she wouldn't be there to protect him.

'That girl would have to turn up at a time like this! . . . He doesn't know what to do now . . . He's ashamed . . . He hardly dares look me in the eyes any longer, and still he hasn't got the guts to get rid of her ...'

There were long silences, during which she stared up at the ceiling.

'Deep down, he's a weakling. ...'

A little later she added:

'Like all men! ... If something does happen to me he'll be desperately unhappy, because he'll be haunted all his life by the fear that it was his fault. ...'

As far as the future was concerned this was probably the truth, but for the present Célita was convinced that Léon would not be too upset if his wife were to disappear from the scene. He would never admit it to himself. He would be bound to repulse such a thought if it ever entered his head. It would none the less sort things out.

He was struggling with the many complications, and, contrary to what one might have supposed, all his worries were bringing him closer to Maud instead of drawing them apart. Who knows? Perhaps he was thinking of her at this very moment, as he waited upstairs for the result of the operation?

Maud had not come, of course. He had left her while she was still asleep; for he spent his nights with her now, at the Louxor, formerly a luxury hotel on the Croisette, which had been converted into furnished apartments a few years ago.

In the afternoons, the girl could be seen sunbathing on her balcony, sipping fruit juice and playing the gramophone.

She had three rooms, bright and gay, with a view of the sea and the beach, and she only came down, wrapped in a gown, when it was time for a bathe.

Was Ketty responsible for what had happened the evening after the article in the *Nice-Matin* appeared, when the club was bursting with people? She had been sitting at a table in the front row with a middle-aged man, who looked, and acted, like a cattle-dealer or a large-scale farmer, and who had already drunk quite a lot.

Wasn't it Ketty's job to make the clients drink? It was time for the second show, and between the two shows Maud had stayed upstairs reading in a wicker chair they had installed in the dressing-room for her.

It was one of those evenings which, for no apparent reason, have a more electric atmosphere than usual, and glasses had been broken at the bar, loud remarks had greeted the flashes which went with Ketty's number.

Ketty had just come downstairs again and was back sitting in the same place, and her companion's large hand, with its prominent veins, was digging into her thigh.

That evening Maud was evidently finding it hard to go into her trance, as they were calling it now that the journalist had used the word in his article, and this was precisely the trouble with her number: it was liable to fall flat if people didn't sense her quivering all over.

She had just knelt down, the upper part of her body naked, and leaning backwards, clasping her breasts in both hands, she began swaying in time with the music, her face looking agonized, her mouth twisted with the effort.

Most of the spectators were taken in, holding their breath, but that evening there were some on whom the charm failed to work, and Maud felt it, as did Gianini, who was making signs at his musicians.

In a minute, half a minute, it would probably all have been successfully over, when Ketty's companion, standing up for a better look, just as he would have done at the local fair, had called out in a croaking voice:

'Want any help, sweetheart?'

Immediately, the spell was broken, and the whole room, torn from the magic, had burst out laughing, while Maud, completely thrown off balance, tried to get up and instead fell awkwardly over on her side.

Léon, red with fury, had rushed forward. He stayed a long time in the dressing-room, where Maud could be heard crying, talking to her the while in a low voice, almost pleading with her. When he came down again, he looked bad-tempered, and, against all the traditions of the house, he had called out in a loud voice:

'Ketty!'

Except for the cattle-dealer, who still sat in his place waiting for her to return, everybody had understood. When Ketty came downstairs again she was wearing her coat, carrying her clothes over her arm, her shoes in her hand, and Madame Florence, to whom her husband had hurriedly whispered something, handed her an envelope already prepared.

'Cheerio, girls!' she allowed herself the luxury of calling out as she left.

That night she had still slept in the rooms she shared with Natasha and the next morning she was gone, avowedly to Geneva, where she claimed they were eagerly expecting her.

From what had been heard since, she had not even attempted to go there; for she had been seen several times on the pavements of Nice, around the Place de la Victoire.

How had Léon managed to remain so calm and collected during all this while, and still find time to devote to his new girl-friend? Everything had happened at once. The very next day Madame Florence entered the clinic and an hour later Léon received a letter asking him to present himself at the police station.

Once again Célita's inspiration had been a bad one, for her telegram had no more produced the desired effect than her telephone call to the police. When Léon went to see him, the superintendent had a long letter in front of him from Maud's mother, insisting on her daughter's return.

What had gone on behind the scenes they had only been able to glean in fragments. The fact remained that it was only once, on the evening after Léon's visit to the police station, that Maud had not appeared in the cabaret, and that the next morning somebody had seen the *patron* entering a lawyer's office.

Ludo, who should know about this sort of thing, had stated:

'As soon as she's eighteen, they can't touch her or the *patron.*'

Two days later Madame Leroy arrived at Cannes and at three o'clock that same afternoon, as she didn't know her daughter's address, she appeared at the Monico, just when the cleaning-women were raising clouds of dust. Émile had spoken to her, and described her to Célita:

'A rather fat little body, dressed in black as if she was in mourning, with a moustache.'

She had just spent quite a while staring at the photograph of Maud in the window and was still boiling with indignation.

'So it's true! She's doing that! My daughter, whom I brought up as a ... as a ...'

She was so comical that it was hard to feel sorry for her, especially since she later asked Émile:

'How much does she get paid, for doing that?'

Émile had telephoned the *patron*'s home to warn him and, getting no answer, next called the clinic, finally the Hôtel de la Poste, where Maud was still living at that time.

'Monsieur Léon? There's a lady here who insists on seeing you ...'

'Let me speak, I'll teach him!' little Madame Leroy burst in, trying to grab the receiver from Émile.

'No, madame ... He's coming round ... It's her mother, *patron* ... I keep telling her you'll be coming, but ...'

Léon was anxious in case Émile had given her Maud's address and within a few minutes he came running up, his tie crooked, though not before he had taken the trouble to ring his solicitor, who duly arrived soon afterwards. Since it was impossible to talk in peace in the club, with the two old women still busy working, the three of them had gone off to the solicitor's home in the Square Mérimée, opposite the Casino.

Nobody knew what passed between them, except that after about an hour Maud had been summoned by telephone and had joined them. What kind of scene had been played there? What bargain had they concluded? Whatever the case Madame Leroy was never seen again at the Monico, and she had taken the train back the same evening.

If the *patron* had any idea who had sent the telegram, he had given no sign of it, and in any case, even without the telegram, Madame Leroy would have heard about it sooner or later, since a Paris weekly published in its next number not one but five photos of Maud, including her 'ecstasy' one, as the paper called it, together with a gossip-story on the 'girl who had found her vocation as a striptease dancer'.

Ketty's departure already left a gap. Madame Florence's absence from the cash-desk caused genuine distress, and they found themselves, to their surprise, talking in whispers, walking around on tiptoe.

The final blow, which seemed to destroy all hope of returning to normal life, was Maud's move to the Louxor and her kind of ceremonial which, from then on, accompanied her arrival and departure. She never turned up now before the stroke of midnight, a few minutes before she was due to go on. The *patron* left the Monico in his car just in time to go and fetch her. From a branch of a famous Paris shop he had bought her a white coat, which, as befitted her new status, she would take off at the door and hand to Francine.

What irritated Célita most was the shy, almost humble manner Maud adopted in the club, both towards the clients and with the other girls and the staff. To everyone she addressed a formal little 'Good evening', as if to apologize for being there at all, then sat down at her table waiting her turn, since she didn't have to change, and never failed to applaud Célita's number, which preceded hers.

'And now, ladies and gentlemen, the management of the Monico have the pleasure and the honour . . .'

She did not always remain in the dressing-room between the two shows; sometimes she went off to the Casino, alone or with the *patron*.

Monsieur Léon, aware that, even looking on the bright side, his wife would be incapacitated for many weeks, if not months, had sent for a sister of his, whom nobody had ever heard of before, a pretty enough woman, a little too fat, a little past her best, but still appetizing, and not unlike him to look at.

She and her husband ran a café at Le Havre, near the docks, and it was noticeable in the way she sat at the till. But from her raucous voice, with its common undertones, and other insignificant details which didn't escape women like the ones at the Monico, they had guessed that once upon a time she had earned her living by other means.

Unlike Florence, she was never heard to say:

'Now, ladies ...'

She called out, with false chumminess:

'Come along, girls ...'

She was on familiar terms with them from the start.

'You, Ginger, it's time you got a move on ...'

'Ginger' meant Célita, while Natasha had become 'Lanky' and Marie-Lou 'Fatty'.

She had one child, a little boy about the same age as Pierrot, and she got on well with Francine; whenever they had a moment to spare, they would be talking about measles and worm powders.

Célita had still not left, had not created a scandal, as Natasha, in particular, had expected and as Ludo feared. She fretted a good deal, certainly, but she was careful to attack neither Léon nor the new favourite, though this didn't mean that she had given in.

Between her and Florence a kind of trust had been established, even a sort of intimacy. Yet during her almost daily visits to the clinic, the two women hardly spoke, probably because they had no need of long phrases to understand each other.

Léon, moreover, was not hiding much from his wife. He even told her more than Célita imagined, and for that reason Florence was the first to bring up the subject of the Louxor apartment.

'I think he was right. He couldn't leave her at the Hôtel de la Poste. Do you realize how unhappy he is?'

Was Florence deluding herself? Was her illness depriving her of her intuition, her woman's instinct, to that extent?

'You don't believe me, but it's the truth. At a certain age men are completely defenceless, even the ones who think they're so well protected; in fact, especially those. It can happen to women too. ...'

She interrupted herself, to scold Célita gently.

'Why did you bring flowers again? He sends me so many

the nurse doesn't know where to put them now. It's salving his conscience, you see? I know he loves me. But it's too strong for him. ...'

After quite a long silence she added:

'You too, you very nearly succeeded ... And with you I'd have been more frightened. ...'

Hearing the *patronne* talk like that, in the muted monotonous voice of a nun, Célita felt disheartened; she was left to carry on the fight alone.

Another day Florence had said:

'He can tell you're all against him, and that hurts him, particularly in your case. ...'

'He said that? He mentioned me?'

Florence gave no details and Célita suspected her of lying, even guessing the motives which prompted the *patronne* to say that to her.

Even had she been in good health, the idea might have occurred to her of their making common front against the enemy, leaving them free to resume the battle against each other, mercilessly, later.

Wasn't that what Célita had imagined she could read in Florence's eyes, the night of Maud's arrival?

Now that she was out of the game, temporarily or permanently, she didn't want Célita to give up.

If anyone was to take Léon from her, whether it was while she was alive or after her death, at all costs it must not be Maud.

'It's tragic, you see, for a man like him to be in a position like this, and so he's miserable. Yesterday he sat there, where you are now, and started crying, holding my hand and asking me to forgive him. ...'

Célita pressed her nails into the palms of her hands to stop herself crying out in fury.

Now, as she waited in the garden with her companions, thinking of the body cut open, up there on the operating-table, she heard again Florence's last words the day before, just as the bell was ringing for the end of visiting hours.

'Off you go! I may never see you again. Don't be too hard on him. One day, you'll see ...'

It was only to her that Florence had spoken like this; didn't it constitute a sort of will? With Marie-Lou, Natasha or Francine she merely asked questions which showed she still took an interest in the cabaret, inquiring how many clients there had been, when they had closed: and presumably Léon's sister, who was called Alice, told her the figure for the takings each day.

Natasha had had a talk with the chief nursing sister, who lived in the same building as she did. She had insisted on discovering the result of the tests, especially to learn whether it was a case of cancer of the uterus, and, without giving a direct answer, the sister had made a vague gesture and uttered a sigh. ...

'What a long time!' Marie-Lou was getting impatient. 'Do you think that's a good sign?'

'Some operations last two or three hours, and even longer,' Natasha replied; she knew a little about everything. 'It depends on what they find. ...'

A little wizened old man, his skull brown with the sun, was leaning on a window-sill on the second floor, wearing the patient's blue-striped dressing-gown, and he had waved at them two or three times.

'Do you know who he is?' asked Célita.

'I feel I've met him somewhere,' Marie-Lou answered.

'I daren't look up to see for sure. Let's walk along to the end of the path and I can have a good look on my way back. ...'

Then she too had given a little wave towards the second-floor window.

'Who is it?'

'You've never seen him; it was before your time. He owns a wholesale grocery business in the rue d'Antibes, with his two sons; both of them are married and have got children. He loves me. I used to call him grandfather and he lapped it up.

'Only a year ago he was still coming twice a week; he had

his fixed days for it. He only drank mineral water because he was on a diet, but he always bought us a bottle of champagne, Lulu and me.

'You never knew Lulu either. She went and got married in Morocco to somebody she met through an advertisement.

'One evening the poor old boy saw one of his sons come in and he rushed off to the cloakroom, where he stayed hiding for nearly two hours. He always left at midnight, whether the show was over or not, because that was the time the café shut, where he was supposed to be playing cards.'

In this way they tried to keep their minds off what was happening behind the frosted-glass windows and each time they passed they paused a moment in front of Ward 6, where the young mother was now giving her baby the breast.

'If Florence died . . .' Marie-Lou began.

'Touch wood!' Francine exclaimed.

And Célita also touched the little twig the other woman had picked up.

'You're right. Let's not think about it. . . .'

But all at once they started thinking about it, not only out of pity for Florence, but because their means of livelihood was at stake. Once Léon was free to do what he pleased, would he carry on with the Monico, and even if he did so, the way he was behaving now, wasn't it likely that he would soon be forced to shut down?

Célita suspected Ludo of following the course of events with special interest and of having his eye on the night club. It might be his opportunity to step into the *patron*'s shoes. He was divorced, his son was grown up and doing his military service. If Célita, in whom he showed a marked interest, were to manoeuvre skilfully . . .

She rejected the thought as soon as it entered her head, not only because now wasn't the time for it, when Florence was lying there with her stomach cut open, but because she knew it would never work.

It was not so much security she was looking for. Security was only of secondary importance. The important thing was that she no longer had any wish to live without a man, that she had decided this man was Léon and that she refused to give up.

There was one person who had seen through her better than her friends, better even than Madame Florence, and, strange as it may seem, this person had never had a proper conversation with her and hardly knew her.

This was the Comte de Despierres, who had been in a lot during the last few days, invariably sitting at the bar, watching the people coming and going with his irritating smile. Célita had got it into her head that he came to see her, since she was always the one he bought drinks for. He asked few questions, and when he did, they were brief and cynical. Was it Ludo, with whom she sometimes saw him gossiping across the counter, who kept him informed?

Once, for example, he had simply asked:

'Not dead yet?'

'Are you speaking of the *patronne*?' she had replied severely.

'That'll still be one of them out of your way, won't it?'

She hated him, and none the less she could not help going over to join him as soon as he beckoned her.

'How are the lovers getting on? No jewels yet?'

'She's too smart for that.'

'Yet, you see, her heart's not set on having that place at the cash-desk.'

'How do you know?'

'I can see through her as well as I can through you. That's all I want.'

'Because you're so intelligent, I suppose? So very superior and intelligent. . . .'

'I'm not sure about that, but I know women. As far as that girl's concerned, she's just using the *patron* of the Monico as a stepping-stone. He can help her over the first step, which is the most difficult. She knows very well she's got to smooth away her rough edges, and before she aims higher she'll need a halo.'

The notion of the halo made her laugh.

'Let's say, if you like, a past which is more or less spicy, a good wardrobe, some jewels, her entrée into the casino, and probably a car into the bargain. . . .'

Célita gazed at him with wide staring eyes, struck by the truth of his remarks, and he went on in a careless tone, like a conjurer condescending to do a few card tricks:

'At thirty-two' – and he pointed his cigarette towards the cash-desk – 'you might fancy that seat over there. Not at nineteen. At nineteen that would be considered sheer burial alive; they imagine they're going to go much further.'

He stubbed out the cigarette in the trade-marked ashtray.

'And she will go further!'

She wondered whether Léon, who was watching them from across the room and frowning, realized that he was the indirect subject of the conversation. Rather than let the Count see that he had impressed her she preferred to murmur nonchalantly:

'I didn't know you went in for fortune-telling.'

She only really understood two days later, when she had to undergo, in her heart of hearts, a humiliating experience.

Curiously enough, the state of nervous excitement in which she had been living since Maud's arrival had been accompanied with a parallel sexual excitement, and one afternoon, when Marie-Lou was on the beach, she had not sent Émile away when he hoisted himself up on to the window-sill from the street.

Émile now had more free time than before, since the *patron* did not call in so regularly at the Monico during the afternoons and was sometimes even seen in a pair of bathing-trunks, lying stretched out next to Maud on the Louxor beach.

Célita suspected that Émile, to save time, got rid of many of his leaflets by throwing them down drains.

He always returned with a piece of news for her; he was the only one who ever went to the Louxor apartment to do errands, and he had found Léon there reading the paper, in his pyjamas, in an armchair on the balcony.

'He didn't seem to mind me seeing him like that, making

himself at home, and he even showed me the bedroom and said:

'"Cosy, isn't it?"'

Émile was no longer so deeply moved when Célita complied with his wishes, but he showed his satisfaction with exuberance.

'Gee, you're a nice sort of a girl! And your skin's so soft!'

Célita, more and more often, aspired to something better. Why didn't the Count, who intrigued and repelled her at the same time, make some move? The idea of making love with him, even though she despised him, did not displease her.

She had many times considered it, telling herself that, since he came back so often and never took any notice of the others, he must have considered it as well.

One evening, to try out the ground, she had murmured, as she lightly pressed her breast against the man's arm, almost inadvertently:

'You're always talking about women and you know such a lot about them. Yet you don't seem to do much about it. . . .'

At once, from the smile which lit up the man's face, from a sense of relief which she detected in him, she had a presentiment of the truth.

'That's just it!' he said, wrinkling his eyelids. 'I have an infinite appreciation for women, and they can be exquisite friends. All my life I've regretted not having a sister. Why, nothing would give me greater pleasure than your coming one afternoon and having a cup of tea with me on the Croisette. . . .'

And then, since she was still at a loss as to what he was implying:

'When did you guess that I was an invert?'

He didn't say homosexual, but used a term which was more elegant somehow, and scientific at the same time.

'You look disappointed?'

'Why should I be disappointed?'

'I could be an excellent friend for you, because you're as complicated a creature as one could wish for, and what

107

fascinates me most about you is that you have all the vices. I once had a friend who ...'

'Thank you.'

'It was meant as a compliment.'

He had realized something had gone wrong, that the spell, if there had been a spell, was broken.

'I'm very sorry. I was mistaken.'

His last words were:

'It's a great pity.'

He did not return to the Monico and Célita preferred not to think about him any more.

'Couldn't we go and ask if it's over yet?' Marie-Lou inquired, anxious to get back to bed.

It was eleven o'clock. Florence had been on the operating-table for nearly two hours. Maud was probably still asleep, or at least reclining in her swing-chair on the balcony, watching the multi-coloured specks of the bathers on the sand and the sails gliding across the bay.

What none of them could guess was that, at that moment, Léon had come out into the corridor, on the first floor, and stopped a nurse as she went by.

'Do you know where I can find a telephone?'

'Try the office on the ground floor.'

There he timidly asked permission to use the telephone, gave the Louxor number, which he knew by heart, and was obliged to speak in the presence of the secretary.

'Is that you? ... Yes ... No, it's not over yet. ... No! Nobody can tell me a thing. ... The door's shut. ...'

His voice became softer, almost a whisper, as he added:

'I shan't be long. ...'

It was said so tenderly that he might just as well have said 'darling'.

'Are you waiting for number seventeen?'

'Yes.'

'Didn't anyone tell you it'll be another hour? If there's anything you've got to do ...'

He was tempted, but resisted. As he walked past the front door, at the foot of the stairs, he noticed the four women waiting in the garden, and, sulkily, he muttered some unkind words at them as if the only reason for their coming was to make him feel guilty.

As he didn't dare to smoke inside, he had been intending to have a cigarette on the steps of the entrance; now he preferred to go without.

It did not take quite an hour, but forty minutes, and the four women were so tired of standing, their feet were so sore, that they had finally sat down on a bench, as if they were in a public garden.

It had never entered their heads that there was another entrance to the clinic, and it was Natasha who heard the surgeon's red car starting up, and Léon's almost immediately afterwards.

'Why don't you go in?'

They sent Célita off to reconnoitre and she made her way to the office, forcing herself not to look into the wards, whose doors were all ajar.

'Are you for number seventeen?'

'Yes, madame.'

'She can't be seen today, and it's not certain yet whether the doctor will allow any visitors tomorrow. I should warn you that it's highly unlikely.'

'The operation?'

The woman in the office, whose job it was to record, in a number of columns, all the births, illnesses, and deaths, looked at Célita as if she had asked something ridiculous.

'It's over, naturally.'

'But . . .'

'She's still under the effects of the anaesthetic and she'll sleep till this evening.'

'Is the doctor at all hopeful?'

Again this word did not seem to have the same meaning for the secretary as it does for ordinary mortals; perhaps it meant absolutely nothing to her, for she simply looked at Célita, her eyes quite expressionless.

'I suppose we oughtn't to send any flowers?'

'Until further notice, certainly not.'

'Couldn't I just see her, even through the crack in the door?'

'Impossible.'

'Thank you.'

She rejoined the others in the garden and the four of them moved off towards the iron gates, where Marie-Lou remembered to wave her hand at the little old man on the second floor.

'Well?'

'Nothing, except that she's alive. They say she'll sleep till this evening.'

'And then?'

Célita merely shrugged her shoulders and Marie-Lou declared:

'As far as I'm concerned, I need a drink before I go and do the same; I'll treat you all.'

In a nearby street they discovered a little bar, where people came in the evenings to play bowls, but which was empty at this time of day. The owner, in his shirtsleeves, had been reading the paper in an easy chair, where the cat had taken his place now that he had been interrupted; he looked in some bewilderment at these unwonted women customers, who all chose vermouth, since he hadn't got their regular drinks.

Marie-Lou, again, had the last word:

'She'll pull through all right, trust me. And before a month's out you'll see her doling me out the fines because the polish on my toe-nails is chipping off or I've been eating garlic. Let's have the same again, Arthur!'

Chapter 2

FOR a long time now, one might say ever since Maud's arrival at the Monico, Célita had been trying to make some sort of contact with Léon but, whether deliberately or not, he was continually slipping away from her. When she arrived in the evening, if he was already there, he nodded to her in the same way as he did to the others, seeming preoccupied, and if, during the course of the night, he had anything to say to her concerning her work, it was brief and to the point.

One afternoon, before Florence had her operation, he had arrived at the clinic while Célita was sitting at her bedside and, after kissing his wife on the forehead, he had gone over to stand in front of the window; he did not move from there for the rest of her visit.

Day after day, she would watch carefully for a chance to get him to herself at last. She had nothing particular to say to him. She was not at present hoping for anything from him, but she could not bear to live with this hostile vacuum between them.

A dozen times she had been on the point of making a scene at the height of the evening's entertainment, and this might have been a relief. She purposely infringed all the sacrosanct rules of the house, under his very eyes, as if to defy him: going out during the show to have a breath of fresh air on the pavement, or again, when she knew she was being watched, refusing to dance with a good client, on the excuse that her feet were hurting her.

She never managed to be alone with him and it would scarcely have helped to go to the Monico one afternoon, since she would have to be very lucky to choose one of the rare days on which he now went there, and, in any case, the cleaning-women would have been there, or the trades-men.

Natasha had left and her absence changed the atmosphere

once again. Probably everybody, Léon included, had rather the feeling that it was the beginning of the end.

Performers had come and gone, of course, replacing each other in more or less rapid succession during the last few years, but that had been due to the normal necessity for a different programme; whereas, this time, it was more like the rats leaving the sinking ship.

For Natasha the whole thing had happened within two evenings, in the most unexpected way. They had all noticed a young man at the bar, very dark, Asiatic-looking, who only knew a few words of French, but, according to Natasha, spoke very good English without the trace of an accent.

She had kept him company until closing time, and after having a snack at Justin's, she had let herself be taken out for a run in a motor-boat with him, just as day was breaking.

The next evening he was there again when they opened, correct and shy, and Natasha had shown the others his photograph, which had recently appeared in the *Nice-Matin*. He was a Persian prince, a genuine one, a cousin of the Shah, who had studied at Cambridge and was now spending a few weeks in France. He had been photographed with the Prefect, who had welcomed him off his plane.

As she was getting dressed for the first show Natasha had announced:

'Guess what he wants me to do? First he asked if I knew Paris well: the Louvre and the museums and all; then he offered me a hundred thousand francs, and all expenses paid, if I would be his guide and interpreter for a month. What would you do, if you were me?'

The Persian had waited for her answer until the second show, smiling, courteous, getting up to offer Natasha a stool each time she went over to join him.

Eventually she informed the others:

'I've said yes, dears. If things were different here, I might have hesitated, but the way the club's going now ...'

'When are you leaving?'

'Tomorrow, by car. He's bought an Italian racing motor and he's already reserved an apartment at the Plaza. ...'

'Have you told the boss the news?'

'Not yet. I'll tell him when I go.'

Would Célita have tried to seize an opportunity like that, if she had known English? Probably. In one go, Natasha was escaping from their world, and they caught themselves looking at her with something like respect.

Immediately after her departure, Léon called Francine as she too was getting ready to go home.

'From tomorrow you'll have to do your number again, for a few days. ...'

Célita and Marie-Lou were already on their way to the Place du Commandant-Maria. They were almost ready for bed when they heard somebody tapping on the shutters. It was poor Francine, very upset, wanting to tell them her news.

She had twice tried to do a striptease number several months before, and Madame Florence had told her, bluntly:

'You'd better stick to the cloakroom, my poor Francine. You make yourself look like a dirty picture.'

It was true. When fully dressed, Francine made the best impression, and without any effort she could pass for a pleasant, attractive little housewife. Once naked, she looked like one of those buxom nudes you see in paintings in art-galleries, her pink flesh forming plump curves, by no means uncomely.

Unfortunately, there was the business of transformation: in other words, the act of taking her clothes off, when, although she did her best to follow the rhythm of the music, everything would go wrong; she became absurd, not to say indecent, and the g-string, whether it was of pink or black satin, appeared erotic and shocking on her rounded belly.

'I couldn't say I wouldn't do it. He seemed so upset. He said that everyone was letting him down and that I was the only one he could depend on. ...'

And to Célita:

'Will you mind if I come round tomorrow, so you can tell me what to do?'

So they had rehearsed a number there, between the un-cleared table and the Henri II sideboard. To replace Francine in the cloakroom, while he waited for a Paris agency to send him a new performer, Léon had hired an old woman with a thin, lugubrious face, who normally sold national lottery tickets round the cafés.

The musicians had taken advantage of the situation to ask for a rise in wages, to which the *patron* had finally agreed, after a violent angry outburst.

And Célita continued to wait her turn to accost him, watching out for a favourable moment.

On Sunday, returning from driving Maud back to the Louxor in his car, he stepped on to the pavement and found himself face to face with Célita, who had ostensibly come out to smoke a cigarette.

'What do you think you're doing here, eh?'

Émile had discreetly moved a few paces away from them.

'I was waiting for you, Monsieur Léon.'

She called him Monsieur Léon as if they were still in the club, not standing outside in the street. Had he any idea that she wanted to make a scene? At all events, he made as if to go straight inside the door, and when she barred his way, there was a resigned look on his face.

'I suppose you want a rise, too?' he muttered a little bitterly.

'No. I simply want your permission to go and see Madame Florence.'

Madame Florence had spent another week in the clinic after the operation and had then been taken home, by ambulance, three days before this. Since then, Célita had not dared go to see her, because she would have been no longer on neutral ground, but in Florence's own home, and Émile was the only one ever to have been inside the flat in the Boulevard Carnot.

Léon looked her sternly in the eyes. He had hesitated, realizing perhaps that he would do better to keep quiet, but his rancour got the better of him, probably because his own conscience was not clear, and he said:

'If you're counting on taking her place, you're wasting your time.'

Then, without waiting to think, without knowing what she was doing, her features hardened and she had slapped him standing stiff on her high heels and he had seized her wrist and twisted it, as she spat in his face:

'Have you no shame? Tell me, aren't you ashamed of yourself?'

It was as if she had regained her real personality, her real temperament.

'And you, you little bitch, weren't you ashamed of yourself when you were doing your level best to try and take her place?'

He spoke low, aware that they were only separated from the customers by a velvet curtain, and still holding her wrist so that he hurt her, he went on, speaking close to her, so close that their breaths mixed, a look of hatred in his face:

'Do you want me to remind you of all the things you've done, all the things you've said?'

At that moment she still regarded him as an equal, but he then uttered a sentence, just one, which forced Célita to close her eyes and give up the struggle:

'*Do you want me to remind you about the gardenal? Do you, you whore?*'

He saw that she was finished and brusquely let go of her, not without giving her a push which almost threw her against the wall.

'Go and see Florence as often as you like, but get any idea out of your head that you'll one day take her place at the desk!'

She didn't burst into tears. Avoiding Émile, who longed for a sign from her so that he could comfort her, she started walking alone towards the end of the street, beside the line of parked cars.

The gardenal business had been a mistake and she had realized as much almost at once, but she had never imagined Léon would have dared throw that in her face, because there were even more unpleasant truths she could fling back at him.

In any case, it was a dirty trick to play and he wouldn't be feeling proud of the way he had just extricated himself.

Didn't that prove what a mess he had made of his life since Maud had got him in her clutches?

It had happened the previous Christmas. At the Monico the party had gone on until half past five in the morning and everybody had had a lot to drink, including Célita, and even Léon, who usually remained sober.

Léon had done something which was quite out of character, since, at any rate at the club, he took his role as *patron* very seriously.

Had Célita looked more desirable than other evenings, or was it the alcohol that made him behave that way? At all events, at four o'clock, at a time when she had no business in the dressing-room, since the shows were finished, he had whispered to her:

'Go upstairs and wait till I come. . . .'

He had in due course gone up to join her there among the costumes lying around untidily, and she had seen an expression on his face that she was more used to seeing on the faces of his clients.

'Our own little Christmas. . . .' he had whispered in her ear, before he took her, the whole time watching the cloak-room below through the fanlight at floor-level.

Had Florence guessed what had been going on when she saw them coming back one after the other? A little later on, she had simply said:

'You'd better fasten your dress properly, Célita.'

The next morning Célita only vaguely remembered how she had got home. A client had driven her off, together with Marie-Lou and another man, and for a long time they had stayed in the car, which he had parked at the end of the jetty, nobody saying a word, the darkness outside blurred by a fine rain.

The way the night had ended had disgusted her, that and now the fact that Marie-Lou, at eleven o'clock, was already up, almost fresh-looking, putting on some scent before going out to lunch, at the Napoule, with a woman friend of hers who was married with children.

She could not get back to sleep, caught in the grip of a

depression such as she had rarely known before. She had never felt so dirty, physically and morally, and though she could not remember anything about it, she knew that if she opened her handbag she would find a crumpled ten-thousand-franc note in it, which she had almost begged from her last partner.

Outside, people were returning home from Mass, families with children walking in front holding each other by the hand, and inside the houses there would be a warm smell of turkey or black pudding.

Marie-Lou, when she left, had forgotten to close the shutters of the dining-room, and through the connecting door, which was ajar, Célita could see from her bed a greyish rectangle of falling rain.

She tried to go back to sleep. Her head ached, her whole body ached; she was ashamed of herself, frightened of the future, seeing no reason why it should be any better than the past or the present.

She twisted and turned in the sheets, and the pillow was clammy. When she had got out of bed to drink a glass of water, she had noticed, on the ledge in the bathroom, the gardenal which she sometimes used.

She took two pills, hoping they would make her sleep at last and stop her thinking, but instead of putting her right out as usual, the drug had plunged her into a state of half-dazedness.

In vain she struggled to sink more deeply into unconsciousness. Each time she returned, not to the surface, but to middle water, water as glaucous and dispiriting as the rectangle of grey rain.

Her thoughts were out of joint, however, though they did not become fantastic as they do in dreams, and they even seemed rational. Since she loathed herself, since life wasn't offering her, nor ever would offer her, anything clean and pleasant, why not simply end it?

At the Monico, Léon had taken her as he might a whore, and what she had done subsequently was to act like a whore again. Was that what she was to become, at thirty-two, now that she no longer had any chance to rise, but every chance of slipping still lower, right to the gutter?

If, instead of two gardenal tablets, she had taken four, or six, or eight ...

She would feel no pain. She would fall asleep, and that evening Léon would realize, too late, what he had lost.

She imagined Marie-Lou's return home, her screams, the demented landlady bursting in, people ringing the police and the doctor, Léon hurrying round in his turn, Florence having pangs of remorse (?) and, later, at the club, the mournful whisperings.

Then there would be the funeral, with the whole staff walking behind the hearse, even the musicians.

The passers-by would stop and say:

'It's that girl who used to dance at the Monico. ...'

Subsequently she had preferred to suppress the memory of that afternoon.

If it hadn't been Christmas, if it hadn't been raining, if she had not got drunk the night before, and if there had not been that episode in the car at the end of the jetty, probably nothing would have happened.

Why, to crown everything, did Marie-Lou have to go out to lunch with a proper family?

Célita was alone in the world, huddled in a not very clean bed, staring at the window, unable to go peacefully to sleep, when she suddenly got an idea into her head, which would have appeared preposterous to anybody in their right senses.

She had taken only two pills, but she might have taken more; nobody could know. When she had thought of dying, hadn't she chiefly wanted to make Léon feel sorry?

It was not so clear as that, but that was still the sense of her reasoning.

If Léon should hear that she were dying, wouldn't she achieve the same result, with the difference that she would be there to profit from it?

It was simple, as long as she planned the details and the setting suitably, and she pondered over it for nearly an hour.

Eventually with her face haggard, seeming to totter, which

demanded no great effort, she had gone to knock on the door of the old landlady who lived alone at the other end of the corridor, and when it opened, she stood propped against the doorpost, in a theatrical pose, speaking with difficulty:

'Please ring Monsieur Tourmaire at once and tell him I'm feeling very ill, that I'm scared I'm going to die. . . .'

At the Monico they practically always used christian names, but Léon did possess a surname.

'Do you know his number?'

'It's in the book. He lives at 57 Boulevard Carnot . . .'

She swayed when she let go her hold on the doorpost and the old lady had to support her as she helped her back to bed.

'Is there anything I could do?'

Yet the landlady had never liked either her or Marie-Lou, because of the underclothes they would hang outside the window, which had been the cause of innumerable squabbles.

'Hello! . . . Monsieur Tourmaire? . . . This is Mademoiselle Perrin's landlady . . . What? . . .'

Célita's surname was equally unfamiliar to him, although he must have read it on her papers. It was better known to Madame Florence, because she had to fill it in every month on the national insurance forms.

'Mademoiselle Célita then . . . She says she's feeling very ill, that she's going to die, and she wants you to come straight away . . .'

That wasn't exactly it. The landlady was talking too much and Célita was beginning to regret her play-acting.

'He's coming. Where is it you feel ill?'

'Everywhere . . . Here specially . . .'

She pointed to her stomach, her abdomen.

'I'll get you a hot-water bottle. . . .'

Léon took scarcely a quarter of an hour to get there and was very alarmed.

'What's happened?'

Indicating the old lady, she murmured in a weak voice: 'Tell her to get out!'

Whereupon, pretending to suffer a spasm, then another,

she pointed at the bottle of gardenal pills which she had placed in full view on the bedside table.

He became still more anxious, but in a different way, as if he were suddenly realizing his responsibilities and the consequences this business might have in store for him.

'I'll call a doctor. ...'

It was plain that he wasn't keen to do so.

'No ... not the doctor. ...' she begged.

She was clinging to the man's large hand as if he alone could prevent her dying.

'I didn't want to fetch you. ... In the end I didn't have the courage to go without seeing you again. ...'

'Have you vomited?'

'No.'

'You must vomit. Get out of bed.'

'I can't ...'

He went and fetched a bowl from the kitchen, made Célita sit on the edge of the bed.

'Stick your finger down your throat ... Right down ... Once more ...'

She obeyed, crimson, her eyes moist.

'Go on ... You've got to be sick ... If you can't manage it, I'll take you along to the hospital ...'

She vomited, bitter liquid for the most part, and he handed her a tumbler of water.

'Drink this and do it again. It'll wash out your stomach ...'

Three times he made her drink and throw up the liquid ...

'I saw them do this once before, in a similar case, one evening in Montmartre; one of the girls had ...'

This memory that now came back to him was to spoil everything. He looked at her more intently, took her pulse, stared at her eyes and lifted her eyelids as he had seen the doctor do.

She had forgotten that a man who had spent much of his life in and out of Montmartre would have seen almost everything.

'How many tablets did you take?'

'I can't remember ...'

She was still striving to win.

'Six perhaps ... Or it may have been only five. ...'

'Or was it just one? Come on, admit it!'

She shook her head furiously.

'Two?'

What could she do but change her tactics and burst into sobs? Since he wasn't going to believe her tale she had better tell him the truth and make it sound pathetic.

'Ever since this morning when Marie-Lou woke me up as she was getting dressed, I've been thinking of you, picturing you at home with another woman, your wife because she was the one who had the luck to meet you when you were still free, while I ...'

He had listened to her right to the end and she had said a great deal more, her breast heaving, carried away by her own game, not really knowing any more when she was being melodramatic and when sincere.

'Every night when I leave you, I watch you going off with her. ...'

She sensed he was weakening, then hardening himself again, only to weaken once more, and it was then that she staked her all.

'I know I'm a bitch. I hate your wife and I shan't be happy till the day she's gone. You want the whole truth? Well, if I could murder her and be sure of not getting caught, I'd do it without turning a hair. I hate myself for it, but I want you and I'd do anything to get you ... Last night, when you had me in your arms, I almost called out to her to come and see us, to show her that you were mine as well as hers, to shout at her that I'm the one you love ... That's what you said, didn't you? ... Answer me!'

Between his teeth, he snarled:

'Little slut!'

And he had slapped her, then flung himself on her viciously.

That day she had not been sure whether she had won or lost. When he was dressed again he was visibly disturbed, and though he had often returned in the course of time, he never referred to what had happened that day.

Had he at last given her the answer just now when he had spat at her:

'*Do you want me to remind you about the gardenal? Do you, you whore?*'

She must calm herself. She would not leave. She would only leave if she was thrown out by brute force, and then it would be the gardenal for good and all, because then she'd have nothing more to lose.

All these cars, some of them worth thousands of pounds, belonged to men, even to married couples, who had paid to see four women take their clothes off, and especially to see Maud perform her dirty little act for them, in which she herself thrilled as she threw men into excitement at the sight of her naked body.

'What I could do to that bitch!' she muttered under her breath, alone in the middle of the pavement.

One day, she was sure of this, she had to feel sure of it, she would have a chance to get her own back, and till then it was essential to keep calm, to preserve complete calm.

'Calm down, Célita, calm down!' she repeated to herself, like an incantation.

And in fact her features did gradually resume their normal expression, she was even able to force a smile for Émile's benefit, when he looked at her, a little frightened:

'Well, did you hear me slap his face?'

Léon did not give her the sack there and then, which meant that he would not do so at all, and consequently that all was not lost.

The very next morning she rang the bell of the Tourmaires' flat, in a prosperous-looking, yellowish-stuccoed house of the type that was built in Cannes fifty years ago. There was a marble staircase, the doors were of a dark wood, fitted with copper handles.

A young girl, not more than sixteen, with untidy hair and a dirty face, opened the door to her.

'I want to see Madame Florence, please. Tell her it's Célita. . . .'

'I'll ask the nurse. If you'll wait in here . . .'

She showed her into a drawing-room with polished furniture of no particular style, which, with its rugs and ornaments, the lithographs and portraits on its walls, its andirons and copper guard in front of the fireplace, might have been the drawing-room of some retired couple with ample means.

Léon and Florence, who had spent most of their lives in the chaos of Montmartre and still lived on the fringe of decent society, were obviously doing their best to establish more reassuring surroundings at home. Heavy drapes framed the windows and through the short muslin curtains one could make out the motionless foliage of the plane-trees in the sun.

A strong-looking woman with masculine features, wearing a white blouse, appeared in the doorway.

'You may go in and see Madame Tourmaire, but please do not stay more than ten minutes, and don't let her talk more than is absolutely necessary, because the slightest effort tires her. ...'

'How is she?'

The nurse put a finger to her lips, pointed to the half-open door, and said in a louder voice, which the sick woman would hear:

'The convalescence is taking its usual course and the doctor is quite satisfied with her progress so far. Now, as always after these operations, it's simply a question of time, patience and will-power ...'

They had started lying to the invalid, and it was a bad sign; Célita sensed this and her heart grew heavy. Yet it was true that a few months earlier she had longed for her death, and would have been capable of carrying out what she had told Léon.

With illness it was another matter, and Célita could not help thinking that one day she might be in her place.

Florence's eyes, in her colourless face, were even larger and more pathetic than at the clinic, and Célita felt a sort of repulsion as she held the hot moist hand which emerged from beneath the sheets to take hers. Most of all she noticed the smell in the room, which was not the smell of medicines, but a human smell which came from the bed and oppressed her to such an extent that she dared not breathe deeply.

'Monsieur Léon gave me permission to come, otherwise I would not have thought of disturbing you.'

'Sit down.'

The voice was from far away. The eyes indicated a cane-seated chair and Célita noticed a crucifix above the bed, which was of walnut wood, in the same style as the wardrobe with two mirrors that stood between the windows.

'I gather you mustn't talk too much and I really only came to tell you that everything's fine at the Monico. Dear old Francine is not doing so badly, some of the clients seem to like her. Yesterday I told her to do a really comic number, but she doesn't dare. We're expecting a new dancer from Paris. . . .'

She was talking for the sake of talking, because Madame Florence's fixed stare disconcerted her. Besides, the nurse was still there in an armchair by the window.

'It's getting hot already, the season's begun, and the Croisette is swarming with tourists, the cars have to just creep along. . . .'

Why did Florence look as though she were laughing at her? It was barely noticeable: the slightest curve of her pale lips.

'You'll be up and about by the height of the summer, when we'll need you more than ever. . . .'

She went on, saying anything that came into her head: 'It's amazing how well Madame Alice gets on. . . .'

Perhaps that was a blunder, since Alice, who was only her sister-in-law, had taken the *patronne*'s place at the desk.

'Though of course it's not the same without you. All the regulars ask after you. You must get well soon. . . .'

She was losing heart. Her thoughts tumbled over each other. Perhaps she was being affected by the idea that this was the room where Léon and Florence slept together.

Suddenly she was feeling further from her ambition than ever, the whole atmosphere was so weird. Émile had said to her:

'They've got a marvellous flat, with carpets everywhere. . . .'

She had not imagined it like this. It was as if she had dis-covered a different Florence, another Léon.

At the Monico they belonged, although on a higher level, to the same sort of group as she did, the same world. With the *patron* in the club or standing at the entrance, and Florence at the cash-desk, the ties which one felt linked them were ties which could be broken.

Here, in spite of the absence of children, they were not only a married couple but a family, and in the black-and-gold oval frames there were two portraits, of an old man and an old lady in clothes of around 1900.

'Is that your mother?' she asked, foolishly.

The woman with the grey hair, done in a tight bun on the top of her head, was wearing a whaleboned bodice and a cameo brooch pinned on her bosom, and had the angular and stubborn features of a peasant.

Florence shook her head and murmured:

'Léon's grandmother; she brought him up, his sister too. ...'

She looked towards the mantelpiece and Célita walked over to it to find a rather blurred photograph of a chubby little boy, holding a hoop in his hand.

'When he was six ...' Florence whispered.

The nurse stood up, indicating that it was time to leave.

'If my visits don't upset you, I'll come and see you again. ...'

She felt Florence wanted to say something to her, but didn't dare, perhaps through modesty, perhaps because of the presence of the nurse.

'Till then ...'

She was accompanied out on to the landing and she was still reluctant to leave; it seemed to her that something had been left undone, she didn't know what, but she felt vaguely un-easy about it.

'May I really come again?' she asked the nurse.

'You had better telephone before you do. We're giving her injections to make her sleep as much as possible.'

In a hardly audible voice she asked again:

'Is there any hope?'

The answer was neither yes nor no. Just a vague shrug of the shoulders.

That night the new girl arrived from Paris, a blonde, with regular features and a body which was more perfect, though less statuesque, than Natasha's. She appeared with a suitcase full of make-up articles and showed her surprise and disappointment when she saw the lack of amenities in the communal dressing-room.

'Aren't there any wardrobes where we can put our things?'

'You've got to hang them on the rod behind the curtain.'

'What about our underclothes?'

Célita showed her the fibre boxes balanced on a plank.

'It looks pretty miserable to me.'

'It is miserable,' Célita agreed.

The new girl called herself Gilda, but her real name was Emma Willenstein, and she had appeared in two or three classy cabarets in Paris; she showed them the programmes.

'Who's the star performer advertised outside? Isn't she here?'

'She only turns up when it's time for her act, and she leaves straight away afterwards.'

Gilda must have lived in France or Belgium for a long time since she spoke French fluently, with an accent which was hard to recognize at first, because, although she had been born in Cologne, her mother was a Czech.

'They told me I could rent the rooms of the girl who has left ... But I don't reckon I'll stay around in this mouldy spot more than a week or two; I've got an engagement for July and August, at Ostend. ...'

That evening everybody's eyes were on her, from the barman to the band, in the way one always watches a newcomer. Célita didn't object when she was told her number would come before Gilda's, which meant a step downwards in the hierarchy for her.

The German girl's dress, of thick white silk, with a skirt as wide as a crinoline, must have cost a lot of money, and her act was studied, a new one for Cannes, because, instead of the traditional g-string, she finished up completely naked, hiding the vital parts with a feather fan which she mimed her readiness to close if the audience demanded it.

Maud applauded, as she had always applauded Célita, and Léon looked across as if to ask her permission to go and congratulate the new recruit in the cloakroom. Anyway, he only stayed there a few seconds, and was soon back leaning against the door as Gianini finished announcing Maud Le Roy, and she, accompanied by a clash of cymbals, advanced on to the floor.

A little later Gilda came downstairs into the room, looked about for Célita, then went and sat at her table. It was rather as if she had just made her choice. For, just as everybody will stare at a newcomer, wondering whether they will like her, the newcomer, for her part, is always a little lost and needs help in getting acclimatized to the club.

'I watched her number through the little window.'

She meant what they called the peep-hole.

'I suppose she sleeps with the boss.'

'Ssh! She's his official mistress. . . .'

'And at the desk, is that his wife?'

'His sister. His wife's ill; she's just had an operation.'

'Funny sort of joint! What's he done all his life?'

'He was a barman in Montmartre for ages.'

'And the fat girl, who looks as though she needs a wash?'

Two or three times during the course of the evening she repeated:

'Funny sort of joint!'

Finally Célita grew so irritated by it that she kept out of her way. In a sense this joint had come to be almost her home and up till quite lately they had really considered themselves members of a family, with a family's loves, hates, jealousies.

Célita knew better than anybody how everything had changed, but it did not make it any less disagreeable to have a stranger taking it upon herself to tell her, looking round the place in her sarcastic, disdainful way.

Anyway, it was plain that she must have come from a funny sort of joint herself, for at about three o'clock in the morning she left the American with the crew-cut and the white linen suit, with whom she had been sitting, and went across to the bar to whisper something in Ludo's ear. Ludo shook his head, sent her over to Monsieur Léon, who was standing near the door, and he also said no to her.

Célita could guess what had happened without having to listen to Gilda, who, with an angry look, had just told her boy-friend.

The new girl had supposed she would be allowed to leave before closing time to accompany the American to his hotel.

The American obviously did not want to sit there drinking champagne while he waited for her, because she wrote something down for him on a piece of paper, which he slipped into his pocket before he left, giving Léon a sulky look as he went by.

Now that the summer holidays had begun, the clients were different, had become noisier and more vulgar; less champagne was consumed and every night there was some customer or other who complained at being charged a thousand francs for a bottle of beer they could buy for a hundred francs in a café.

'Don't forget there's a floor show,' Jules would start explaining each time, and some of them would take their revenge on him by not giving him a tip.

Francine was talking of taking a month off to go with her little boy to the mountains.

The club was slowly emptying. It was half past three. Célita sat alone at a table, thinking of nothing in particular, vaguely watching Marie-Lou yawning while a white-haired man chattered to her incessantly, at the same time busily kneading her fat thigh with his hand.

At one moment the light seemed to fade, a thing which often happened when there was a storm in the mountains.

A few minutes later the telephone rang on the cash-desk and Alice lifted the receiver. At first it seemed that she could not hear because of the music, then she glanced over towards the door. Nor could what she was saying be heard either, certainly not by Célita, who was sitting near the band; but she saw Alice hesitate, then get up and pass behind Ludo, to whom she whispered a few words.

Ludo, frowning, looked from the *patron* to Célita, while Alice leaned over the counter at the end of the bar, to speak to her brother, whom she had beckoned over with her hand.

Célita did not move, held her breath, not missing anything that was happening, and when she saw the *patron* rush outside without his hat, without a word to anybody, she felt her hands turn icy cold.

Her eyes must have been eloquent; through the crowd, the noise, the streamers hanging from the ceiling, Ludo understood her unspoken question, answered her with a movement of his eyelids as he took hold of a bottle of brandy and poured himself a full glass.

Madame Florence was dead.

Chapter 3

THERE had been a violent storm the previous night and the air was clean and transparent, so that in the far distance every detail of the mountains was visible, the little white houses standing out in relief as in stereoscopic views; at a very early hour some of the residents of La Californie and Le Cannet had been able to see Corsica, whose peaks made a jagged line in the merging turquoise blue of sea and sky.

At a quarter to ten it was already hot and hazy, and women in shorts were coming down the Boulevard Carnot, towards the market, glancing curiously at the little groups of people standing under the plane-trees, aware that something was going to happen; but not until they reached No. 57 did they discover the black drapes with the fringes and silver drops. Some of the women crossed themselves.

The people waiting were mainly men, proprietors of cabarets or bars from Juan-les-Pins, Nice, and also from the other side of the Estérel: Saint-Raphael, Saint-Tropez, Toulon, and Marseilles; most of them looked lost at being up and about so early, and some of the faces seemed familiar, as if they had appeared in the papers, in odd items of local news.

Célita arrived with Marie-Lou and Francine and they joined Ludo, Jules, and Gianini on the pavement.

'Have you been upstairs?'

Ludo nodded and they in turn went into the house, as each of the others had done before going out to wait in the street; they climbed the staircase, stopping on the second landing, a little out of breath. The door was shut. Célita felt her bag heavy in her hand, a rectangular bag as big as Madame Florence's, which was a kind of sign of her profession; for whenever she did not go home to the Place du Commandant-Maria for the night, it could hold all her toilet articles and even a nightdress.

Since she was hesitating, Marie-Lou gave her a little shove

and they went through into the passage, where a dim electric light was burning and there was a smell of hot wax and flowers.

The bedroom, where the curtains had been drawn across the windows, was hung in black. The bed and the wardrobe with the mirrors had been removed; there was nothing left but a stand of some sort, covered with a cloth – perhaps the Henri II table from the dining-room? – supporting the oak coffin with its heavy silver ornamentation.

Each of the two women dipped a twig of box in the holy water and made the sign of the cross in the air, then stood there motionless, as if praying, their lips moving, not daring to look around too much.

Several dark figures were disclosed in the dancing light of the candles: Monsieur Léon, his sister Alice, a man who was presumably her husband, two women they didn't know and a little, shrunken old lady, who looked like a church chair-attendant.

It was Florence's mother, who had never been mentioned at the Monico, but had now come down from her village in Berry where she made cheese from the milk of her goats.

They could not see Maud there. Nobody knew whether she would be at the funeral. As they went out, they touched Léon's hand, mumbling some unintelligible syllables meant for condolences, and they were almost surprised to find the sun shining outside and the noises of the street.

Marie-Lou and Francine, who suspected nothing, were left wondering when Célita said to them:

'I'll be back in a minute.'

They watched her almost run to the corner of the street and disappear into a bar.

'What's bitten her?'

'I don't know,' Marie-Lou replied. 'The last two days she's been up and down the whole time, crying one minute, laughing out loud the next, and then not saying a single word, as if she were hiding something.'

And Francine sighed:

'She's always been so melodramatic.'

They would surely have been still more anxious had they seen Célita hurriedly swallow two glasses of cognac, while keeping an eye on the street.

The day after Madame Florence's death the telephone had rung about four o'clock in the afternoon, and Célita had answered it while Marie-Lou went on eating; they had just sat down to lunch.

'Yes, speaking . . .' she said, with surprise.

At the other end of the line a voice she had not recognized had mysteriously announced:

'This is Mademoiselle Motta. Do you remember me?'

'No.'

'You saw me yesterday. I was the nurse who was looking after Madame Tourmaire. Are you alone?'

Célita had hesitated, then answered: 'Yes.'

'I've been asked to give you a message and I wanted to do it without saying a word to anybody else. A few minutes before she died Madame Tourmaire muttered:

'"Tell Célita that I'm depending on her. . . ."

'When I asked her what she meant, she added:

'"Just tell her that, she'll understand."

'That was all. I've given you the message. It was my duty, I suppose.'

She had hung up and Célita had told Marie-Lou nothing when she looked at her inquiringly. Ten minutes later, however, as if a thought had been pursuing her the whole time, she had exclaimed:

'It's fantastic!'

'What is?'

'Nothing. You wouldn't understand, and anyhow it's too late!'

'Too late for what?'

'Nothing, Marie-Lou, you fool. Forget it!'

From that time on she had become strange. At times she would stare in front of her as if she were seeing things nobody else could see, and she wore the appearance of a sleep-walker.

Francine was right: Célita had always been melodramatic,

not only with other people, but with herself, and it was probably true that she needed to play certain roles, or exaggerate her own, because she could not put up with life as it really was.

Nobody could have any inkling of her decision, or know that all that was happening now at 57 Boulevard Carnot, and the ceremony of prayers of intercession for the deceased which would shortly take place, with the organ and incense, in the dimly lit church, followed by the funeral procession across the town, was but the prologue to a final scene which Célita, and she alone, had planned, since it was the only one, in her eyes, that was possible.

Had Madame Florence had any idea that her message would arrive too late? Célita had held out as long as possible; the situation could still have been saved when she had slapped Léon in the street, with Émile looking on. But not now.

There were certain things he should never have said. He had not thrown her out, but even that was a sign of his contempt, and all the more unbearable in that it meant he was simply not bothering to do so, because he was convinced that she would end up by walking out of her own accord. Who knows? Perhaps, by waiting, he had grown angry that she was still there, as a kind of witness?

Maybe he would get tired of Maud, as Florence had apparently believed, or else, as Ludo had predicted, Maud would be the one to leave, to climb one further rung of the ladder, as soon as she had the opportunity. In any case that would take weeks, even months, and whatever the final outcome, Léon would only loathe Célita all the more.

He was the one she hated, because she had humbled herself in vain to get him in her clutches, because he despised her for doing so, never realizing that Maud's game was even more disgusting.

Yet it would have to be on Maud that Célita would have her revenge, convinced as she was that this was the best means to hurt him, to make him suffer for a long time, to force him to remember her for the rest of his life.

She knew that if she had spoken to anybody of what she

133

was about to do, nobody would have believed her capable of it, not even Marie-Lou, who lived with her.

For three days she had been growing more excited, on her own, almost cold-bloodedly, one might say, and things were not necessarily all so gloomy, in the future she was planning for herself; she was still capable of calculations, even of fairly cynical calculations.

Once Maud Le Roy was dead, Célita would be put in prison, of course, and it would be an enormous relief for her to find peace at last between four walls and not to have to think any more. Whilst she foresaw, in this way, the consequences of her action, she was concerned about its external repercussions, the reports in the newspapers, how the people at the Monico would be dumbfounded, and above all, the way Léon would react.

Wouldn't he realize, at last, that the episode the previous Christmas had not just been a poor piece of play-acting?

They would not condemn her to death, for this would be a *crime passionnel* if ever there was one. If she weren't acquitted – and she had not much hope of that – she would get away with a not very long term, five years perhaps, and the chances were that Léon would come and visit her while she was in prison.

Célita allowed herself a smile now and then, at the thought that she was after all going to carry out the *patronne*'s dying wishes, though in a way Madame Florence had not foreseen.

The material preparations had taken two days. She knew that it would be impossible, without formalities which were out of the question for her, to buy a revolver at a gunsmith's, and she could not think of anyone to borrow one from. But she knew where to find one, at the Monico, of all places, in one of the drawers of the cash-desk, where Léon had put it last autumn after there had been armed robberies at two establishments on the Riviera.

The club was closed. The show-case with the photographs of the naked girls had been taken away temporarily and a black-edged notice announced: 'Closed owing to bereavement.'

She had telephoned several times. Now that the *patron* had stopped going to the club regularly every afternoon, Émile had been given a key, so that he could open it for the charwomen and the delivery men.

For a day and a half, the telephone had kept ringing with no reply, and she didn't know Emile's address at Le Cannet. Nor did she see him on the Croisette, where she looked for him, because he had given up distributing the leaflets.

The second day, about six in the afternoon, after having already telephoned in vain at four, she pushed the door on the off-chance, and it had opened, almost knocking over Émile, who had been squatting down to pick up the letters the postman had pushed through the slit in the door.

'It's you!' he said, surprised, as he stood up.

'I've come to collect one or two things I need.'

'It's lucky for you the boss just sent me over to collect the letters. I hardly got here a minute ago. . . .'

The shutters were closed and it was dark, which was lucky too, for Célita was not sure how best to play her role.

'I'm going upstairs for a moment. . . .'

Then, just as she was pushing open the door with the peep-hole:

'You wouldn't go and buy me a packet of cigarettes, would you?'

She could not think of any other ruse to be rid of him and she sighed with relief when, not suspecting a thing, Émile went off whistling.

She had brought a screw-driver in case the drawer was locked, as it probably would be. The tobacconist's was not far and Émile always walked quickly.

The lock gave way immediately; nobody had thought of removing the short-barrelled revolver which she hurriedly hid in her bag.

She had not had time, however, to leave the bar, and as Émile came in, she picked up a bottle of whisky.

'Any objection?'

'Of course not.'

'Do you want some?'

'You know spirits burn my stomach, even wine does.'

He watched her climb the stairs to the dressing-room, and then return with a frock over her arm.

'Mademoiselle Célita ...'

'I'm in a hurry, Émile. ....'

'It's not what you think. ....'

'I know ... I'll see you tomorrow. ....'

And she did see him, as he greeted them but did not dare to join their group. The motor hearse drew in front of the house, the undertaker's men climbed the stairs and reappeared carrying the coffin on their shoulders.

'Do you think she'll come?'

Célita, suddenly furious, looked at Marie-Lou, who of course could not understand how her entire plan was based on Maud's presence at the funeral.

Léon came out through the door, dressed in black, with a stiff, very white collar, and a black tie which gave him the air of a head waiter and revealed for the first time – God knows why – that his nose was slightly crooked and one eye was higher than the other.

Beside him trotted the little old lady with the wrinkled face, then, together, came Alice, her husband, and Maud, also in black, even to a black hat and gloves, looking like a member of the family.

They waited a little longer, out in the sunshine, while people in the street stopped to watch them form up into a procession. Ludo, Gianini and the musicians took their places, Émile, without losing sight of Célita, sidled in beside old Jules, and then, haphazardly, came Léon's colleagues, who all knew each other, some tradesmen, equally acquainted, amongst them, and a few strangers.

The parish church was at the top of the boulevard, but Léon had insisted that the service take place at Notre-Dame, near the Monico, probably because it was the town's fashionable church. The hearse was laden with wreaths and one of them, for which a subscription list had been sent round, bore a card with the words:

136

To our dearly departed employer
THE STAFF

It had been Ludo's suggestion; he knew the way things were done.

Léon, hat in hand, walked with his head lowered, and Célita noticed that his hair was already getting thin. Maud was just behind him, and like Alice's, her eyes were red and from time to time she dabbed at her face with a handkerchief, while the little old lady, for all that she was the dead woman's mother, looked about inquisitively at this town she had not seen before, which she was unlikely to have the opportunity to revisit.

Célita was calm, a little tense, but calm. She had been thinking very hard. Now that she had made her decision and had predicted the slightest detail which might occur, it was almost as if she were no longer concerned with the business at all, as if she had set going a mechanism that would now work without her, and like Florence's mother, she found herself staring at things in the street, then at the church as they entered it, the same church from which, not so long ago, she had watched a bride leaving.

The two charwomen, Madame Blanc and Madame Touzelli, were already there, kneeling in the pew second from the back, and you could see they were used to it. Marie-Lou also knew when to cross herself, genuflect, stand up or sit down, have her collection money ready, and Célita watched her, in order to follow her example.

There was no Mass, only a service of intercession, and the church was more than half full; when they left, people pressed forward on both sides of the porch, almost as inquisitive as at a wedding.

Célita found it all rather unreal, like a painting, or more like a film when the sound-track suddenly fails. She could hardly recognize Léon in his mourning clothes, a suit he had bought ready-made, which was too tight across the shoulders. He was starting to get a pot-belly. He had cut himself shaving and there was still a little red mark on his cheek.

She preferred not to look at Maud, whom the people walking in front of her concealed most of the time, for she wasn't tall. The hearse drove very slowly and the cortège made its way towards the Carnot bridge, blocking the traffic for a while, then went along the rue de Grasse, climbing slowly towards Les Broussailles, where the cemetery was situated, not far from the new hospital.

There were fewer people than there had been on the way to the church, and two men left the procession to rush off to a bistro for a quick drink, and then returned to their places, wiping their mouths.

'Do you believe in heaven and hell?' Marie-Lou asked out of the blue, impressed by the intercession service.

Célita did not answer the question, but found it had a slightly disturbing effect. She preferred not to think about it, particularly now.

She was past going back. Her pride in herself was at stake. She had envisaged every possible outcome and there was no time to go over it again.

'I often wonder ...'

'Shut up, will you?'

She had said it so harshly that Marie-Lou and Francine looked at her with astonishment. They should have learnt to expect almost anything from her.

They were approaching too fast, now, along streets which became more and more empty, with the splash of colour made by a local shop only appearing at rare intervals.

She refused to ask herself why she had taken her decision. She had just *had* to, and that was that! She would do it whatever happened. She could feel the weight of the revolver in her handbag and nothing else mattered to her any more.

She glimpsed Maud's face as she turned round to look at the procession and for an instant their eyes met. Strangely enough Maud was the first to look away, embarrassed. Had she persuaded Léon to give Célita the sack? If that were achieved, she would no longer have any enemies left at the Monico, since Marie-Lou and Francine hardly counted. They were soft stuff. In any case Francine had just told them that it was fixed, she was going away for a month, with Pierrot, to the mountains, and she wasn't sure whether she would return to the Monico. A businessman from Grasse, who came to see her once or twice a week, and whom Pierrot already called 'uncle', was eager to set her up and keep her permanently.

The women's heels twisted on the uneven cobblestones of the rising street; they passed in front of old villas, large mansions which had known their heyday when Cannes was still a winter resort and were now converted into flats. The cross, carried by a choir-boy, wavered above their heads and they were now approaching the cemetery, were passing in front of brand new tombstones, stacked along the pavement. The priest began to chant his prayers again.

'What's the matter?'

'Nothing. I nearly fell.'

It was true. Her head was going round as if she were on a swing at the fair, everything she saw was becoming blurred in the sun.

They followed some well-trodden paths, then more recent ones, and the procession stopped not far from a wall, the cross silhouetted against the sky at the end of its long black wooden pole, and in the midst of the dark figures there appeared a rectangular hole in the yellowish earth.

She had to do it, that was all!

She had thought things over beforehand. Later she would perhaps think things over again. For the moment she had ceased to exist.

She only knew that she must slip between two men who were standing in the front row, since she had decided to do her deed at the very moment when the coffin had been lowered and Léon was throwing in the first shovelful of soil.

'Sorry . . .' murmured one of the men she was pushing, as he stepped back to make room for her.

Maud was in full view, opposite her. She had taken her place next to Léon, as if to be ready to comfort him with a squeeze of his hand.

The grave-diggers had begun work, their faces sweating,

and the coffin was being lowered, supported by ropes, stopped for a moment as if it had met an obstacle, then started falling again.

Célita opened her bag with her right hand; it disappeared inside, feeling the revolver, seizing the grip.

Nobody was taking any notice of her. She would have time to take aim. Barely three yards separated her from Maud and there was no obstacle between them.

'*Libera me, Domine . . .*'

The liturgical phrases became but a murmur as they were drowned by the noise of a concrete-mixer somewhere outside the cemetery.

Célita's clammy hand still clasped the grip of the revolver in her bag, her index finger probed, searched for the trigger, found it.

She stared at Maud, suddenly bewildered, as if she were no longer conscious of where she was or what she was doing. Did she even still know who the young girl was who was looking down into the hole and why she was going to kill her?

Somebody handed Léon a shovel, with a little earth on it, and he bent down awkwardly, while Célita, noticed by nobody, took the revolver from her bag.

But now it was not Maud at whom she aimed. She raised the gun slowly, the muzzle turned towards herself; panic had overcome her, there was no other solution but to kill herself.

All she had to do was to raise her arm slightly, turn her wrist. Then it would be over. There would be no more problems, no more unpleasantness nor humiliation, no more Célita, nothing any more.

Léon was straightening up again, his face crimson, looking about him, wondering if there was anything else he had to do, and his eyes rested on Célita, on the gun she was holding in her hand.

Then, without thinking, without realizing how theatrical her action would seem, she threw the revolver into the grave and, pushing through the crowd, began running down the paths, convinced she was being chased, searching for the way out; when she found it, she started off down the steep road leading to the town, her eyes mad.

Chapter 4

MARIE-LOU was the only one of the old lot left; Francine had gone the day after the funeral and they had had one new girl from Marseilles, then another, an Italian whose name could not be announced on the bills because she hadn't yet got her work permit.

Alice, the *patron*'s sister, had returned to Le Havre because her husband needed her, and a former cashier from the Café des Allées had been engaged.

Léon continued to fetch Maud and take her back after her performance: he was living altogether at the Louxor now, going only occasionally to the Boulevard Carnot to collect his belongings.

It was Ludo who got indirect news of Célita and passed it on to Marie-Lou. The fat girl had taken the Italian to share the flat in the Place du Commandant-Maria, because it was too expensive for her alone.

'She's been seen at Nice,' he told her one evening. 'Apparently she was in a small bar, with Ketty ...'

Marie-Lou was too upset to say anything, because for her, and for Ludo as well, those words could mean only one thing.

A few days later a regular client was also to mention her: he had seen her standing in a doorway, near a hotel.

The season was in full swing. The motor-cars were almost bumper to bumper, taking an hour to drive along the Croisette, and women even appeared in the rue d'Antibes in bikinis; Marie-Lou had met a woman who was at least sixty, wearing one in the chemist's.

The end came, as they learned from the newspaper, a few days before 15 August.

The body of an entirely naked woman, covered with bruises 'which might have been due to its being repeatedly buffeted against the rocks', had been recovered from the sea between Nice and Villefranche.

Two days later, the *Nice-Matin* announced that the corpse had been identified as that of 'one Céline Perrin, single, aged thirty-two, born in Paris, rue Caulaincourt, cabaret dancer, who had been summoned twice by the police during the last few days, for soliciting on the streets'.

Finally:

'Investigations are being carried out in certain special areas of the town, particularly amongst North Africans, because the dead woman's handbag and clothes have not been found, and three days before the discovery of the body Céline Perrin had been seen in the company of an Arab whose description is in the hands of the police.'

'Do you think she'd do that, Ludo?'

The barman looked at Marie-Lou without replying, sighed, took a bottle of cognac from the shelves and poured himself a full glass, exactly as he had done for Madame Florence.

'Give me some too.'

Then she began to say:

'If she did that, I think she . . .'

But what was the use of talking?

She emptied her glass in one gulp, because the *patron* was making signs to her to go and change for her number.

12 June 1957